Are Elections Ever Fair

Jessica thought she heard footsteps on the stairs. She quickly pushed the poster back under Elizabeth's bed and hurried out of the room.

Passing the stairs, she almost bumped into Steven heading for his room. He grinned at her. "What are you doing—spying on the opposition?"

Jessica laughed nervously. "Don't be silly. I just thought I'd left a sweater in there. I was looking for it."

"Yeah, sure," Steven said. "Is it time to set up the battle stations yet?"

Jessica rolled her eyes. "It's not a battle, it's a campaign." With that, she tossed her head and went toward her room. But before she went in, she looked back at Steven.

"Uh, Steven," she said, "do me a favor, okay? Don't tell Elizabeth I was in her room."

SWEET VALLEY TWINS

Tug of
War

Written by
Jamie Suzanne

Created by
FRANCINE PASCAL

A BANTAM SKYLARK BOOK®
TORONTO · NEW YORK · LONDON · SYDNEY · AUCKLAND

RL 4, 008–012

TUG OF WAR

A Bantam Skylark Book / December 1987
4 printings through May 1988

Skylark Books is a registered trademark of Bantam Books,
a division of Bantam Doubleday Dell Publishing Group, Inc.
Registered in U.S. Patent and Trademark Office and elsewhere.

Sweet Valley High® and Sweet Valley Twins are
trademarks of Francine Pascal

Conceived by Francine Pascal

Produced by Daniel Weiss Associates, Inc.,
27 West 20th Street, New York, NY 10011.

Cover art by James Mathewuse

ISBN 0-553-15663-2

Published simultaneously in the United States and Canada

Bantam Books are published by Bantam Books, a division of Bantam
Doubleday Dell Publishing Group, Inc. Its trademark, consisting of the
words "Bantam Books" and the portrayal of a rooster, is Registered in
U.S. Patent and Trademark Office and in other countries. Marca
Registrada. Bantam Books, 666 Fifth Avenue, New York, New York 10103.

PRINTED IN THE UNITED STATES OF AMERICA

O   13 12 11 10 9 8 7 6 5 4

To the children of the Mid-Continent Public Library of Independence, Missouri, with thanks for being such wonderful fans.

One

◇

"Those cookies look super!" Elizabeth commented. She could practically taste Amy Sutton's chocolate chip cookies just by looking at them.

"Thanks," Amy said. She turned to see what her best friend Elizabeth Wakefield had brought. Carefully, Elizabeth opened the big white box she had set on the teacher's desk.

"Oh! Cupcakes!" Amy exclaimed.

"It's my mother's special recipe," Elizabeth said. "Chocolate cupcakes with peanut butter frosting and melted chocolate chips. We call them Wakefield Specials."

The two girls looked around to see what the other kids in the class had brought. "There's so much food," Amy murmured in awe.

Elizabeth nodded. "I don't know what to try first!" Platters of cookies, doughnuts, and little sandwiches covered the desk. There seemed to be enough food in the room to feed the entire Sweet Valley Middle School, not just one sixth-grade social studies class.

"I can't believe the Hairnet's actually letting us have a party in class," Amy whispered.

Elizabeth giggled. Her twin sister Jessica called Mrs. Arnette that, too—because the teacher always wore a hair net over her bun. She definitely wasn't the type to let her class have a party for just any old reason.

But this party wasn't just for any reason. It was Linda Lloyd's last day at Sweet Valley Middle School. Linda was the sixth-grade class president.

"Are you excited about moving to Texas, Linda?" Elizabeth asked the rosy-cheeked girl.

"Oh, sure," Linda replied, her normally twinkling eyes a little sad. "But I hate leaving Sweet Valley."

Elizabeth could sympathize with her. She thought Sweet Valley was the most perfect place in the world, and she'd hate to be moving away. But she tried not to let her feelings show—it might only make Linda feel worse. "I'm sure you'll like Texas," she said encouragingly.

"I guess so," Linda replied. "But I feel awful about leaving school in the middle of the year."

"We'll have to elect a new class president," Amy remarked.

"That's right," Elizabeth said thoughtfully. "I wonder who it could be. You're not going to be easy to replace. We'll have to find someone really special."

Linda turned to Amy. "Maybe *you* should run for class president."

Amy's pale blue eyes were laughing. "No thanks! It's too much work for me. Besides, I'm not a born leader."

Elizabeth knew what Amy meant. Her best friend was a great organizer and planner, but she liked working behind the scenes. And it *would* be a lot of work, too. Elizabeth was student council treasurer, and that kept her pretty busy. Being class president, she thought, would probably take even more time.

Even with all that food, there was hardly anything left by the time the party was over. When the bell rang, Elizabeth noticed one last cupcake. She wrapped it up in a napkin and carried it with her as she and Amy walked down the hall to the cafeteria.

"It's too bad Linda has to leave," Amy remarked. "She's been doing a really good job as president. Remember how she organized the canned-food drive for Thanksgiving?"

Elizabeth nodded. "I don't know who's going to be able to take her place." She wondered if *she* had the ability to fill Linda's shoes. She tried to imagine herself as president, making decisions that would affect the entire sixth grade.

"What are you thinking about?" Amy asked.

"Oh, nothing," Elizabeth said, quickly pushing the daydream out of her mind. She couldn't even imagine that anyone would nominate her. And even if she was nominated, she didn't know if she could win.

The cafeteria was crowded by the time Amy and Elizabeth arrived. They waited until they got their lunches, then Elizabeth scanned the crowd for her twin sister.

Her heart sank when she saw Jessica sitting with Lila Fowler and Ellen Riteman. Lila was one of the richest and snobbiest girls in school, and Elizabeth didn't like her very much. Ellen was a snob, too—not as rich or as smart as Lila, but just as nasty. Like Jessica, they were members of the Unicorn Club, and they thought themselves to be as special and beautiful as the mythical animal.

"Do we have to sit with them?" Amy asked as Elizabeth started toward their table.

"I want to give Jessica her cupcake," Elizabeth explained.

As they approached, Elizabeth thought that looking at Jessica was just like looking into a mirror. They had the same long, blond hair, the same blue-green eyes, even the same dimple in the left cheek.

But though they looked identical, the Wakefield twins were very different.

Lots of people thought of Elizabeth as the serious one. That wasn't exactly true—she liked having fun with her friends. But she also liked having time alone, by herself, to read, or write, or just think.

Jessica, on the other hand, never liked being alone. She wanted lots of friends around her all the time, and she wasn't very interested in anything serious, especially school. Mainly she liked having fun—and her idea of fun sometimes got her into trouble. And she always counted on Elizabeth to get her out of it.

The twins had different friends, different interests, and different personalities. But they were still the best of friends.

"I brought you something from the party," Elizabeth said, handing the cupcake to Jessica.

"Thanks," Jessica said. She turned to Lila and Ellen. "They had a party for Linda Lloyd in the Hairnet's class. She's moving to Texas this week," Elizabeth added. "This is her last day at school."

"Which means we have to elect a new class president," Amy chimed in. "There's going to be a special assembly later this week for nominations."

"It's too bad Linda has to leave," Elizabeth said. "I like her."

Lila tossed her head. "*I'm* not sorry Linda's leaving. I don't know how a girl who's not even a

Unicorn got elected in the first place. At least now we've got another chance to fix that."

"Yes, we have to elect a Unicorn," Ellen echoed.

"Oh, absolutely," Jessica said. "But who?"

"I'm not sure yet," Lila said thoughtfully.

Elizabeth didn't think a Unicorn would be a good class president. Even though her own sister was a member, she thought most of the girls in the club were too self-centered. It was her belief that a class president should be someone who cared about everyone—not just the people in one little private group.

Another sixth grader, Jim Sturbridge, ambled over to their table and sat down.

"Who are you girls gossiping about this time?" Jim asked.

"We're not gossiping," Jessica informed him. "We're talking about the sixth-grade class president. Linda Lloyd's moving away, and we have to elect a new one."

"We think the new president should be a Unicorn," Ellen said.

"Oh, yeah? Well, I think the president should be a boy."

"Really?" Jessica asked. "Do you have anyone particular in mind?"

"How about him?" Jim asked. He pointed to a thin boy with glasses standing in the aisle, looking for a place to sit. Lila and Ellen started giggling again, and Jessica joined them.

Elizabeth didn't laugh. The boy Jim was pointing at was Randy Mason. There was nothing really wrong with Randy. He was just terribly shy and studious. He always seemed to be more interested in computers than people. Jessica thought he was a nerd, and even Elizabeth had to admit he wasn't the type to be elected class president.

"Maybe I'll nominate him," Jim said, laughing. "Hey, Randy!"

Randy turned and peered over his glasses at Jim. He looked surprised, and Elizabeth couldn't blame him. Jim had probably never spoken to him before.

Jim got up from his chair and walked over to Randy. "How would you like to be nominated for class president?" he asked, standing over him, grinning wickedly.

The Unicorns were practically in convulsions, hiding their faces behind their napkins. Randy didn't seem to notice, though. He just looked at Jim as if Jim were seriously considering nominating him.

"I wouldn't mind at all," he said politely.

Jim was so startled by this response that he just stared at Randy.

"Excuse me," Randy said, turning away.

Jim made a face at him behind his back. "What a jerk," he muttered as he sauntered away.

Poor Randy, Elizabeth thought. He didn't even realize that Jim had been making fun of him. But all thoughts of Randy Mason flew out of her head as

Julie Porter came running up to their table. Her huge brown eyes were sparkling with excitement.

"Hey, you guys, guess what? Mr. Bowman says the sixth grade gets to run the next book fair!"

"Great!" Elizabeth declared.

Lila looked bored. "Is that all?"

Ellen made a face. "Big deal."

"It *is* a big deal," Julie insisted. "Because that means the sixth grade gets to decide what to do with the money we make!"

Lila actually began to look interested. "Really? Those book fairs can make a lot of money."

"No kidding," Julie said. "Sometimes two or three hundred dollars."

Jessica's eyes widened. "Two or three hundred dollars? And we get to use the money any way we want?" From the expression on Jessica's face, Elizabeth could tell her sister was already thinking of ways to spend it.

Ellen turned to Lila. "What do you think we should spend it on?"

"Wait a minute," Amy objected. "It's not your money. It belongs to the whole class." She looked at Julie. "Who gets to decide what we do with the money?"

"I'm not sure," Julie said. "Mr. Bowman told me to get some ideas from people. I guess he'll pick the best one. Or maybe we'll have a vote."

"I've got an idea right now," Jessica said.

Elizabeth laughed. "I don't think Mr. Bowman's

going to let you spend the book fair money on new clothes."

"Oh, Lizzie, don't be silly. Honestly, I've got a great idea, and it's something for the whole sixth grade." She paused dramatically. "I think we should spend the money on an incredible party."

Elizabeth wasn't at all surprised to hear Jessica's suggestion. There was nothing her twin liked better than a good party, and she'd look for any excuse to have one.

Lila nodded in agreement. "I think that's an excellent idea."

"Perfect," Ellen said.

"I'm not so sure," Amy said slowly. "If the money's coming from the book fair, don't you think we should spend it on something to do with books?"

"OK," Jessica said. "How about a costume party? We can all go dressed as characters from our favorite books."

"A party would be nice," Elizabeth admitted. "But I think Amy has a point. Maybe the money should be spent on something more important—like something for the library."

Jessica made a face. "You mean, spend it on books? The library's already got tons of books."

"That's so boring, Elizabeth," Lila said, shaking her head.

"It doesn't have to be spent on books," Elizabeth said, suddenly getting an idea. She turned to Julie. "Remember in English, when Mr. Bowman said he wished we had a VCR so he could show a tape of the Shakespeare play that was on television? We could use the money to buy a VCR!"

Lila and Ellen groaned.

"That's so . . . so educational," Jessica complained. "I think the money should be used for something fun."

"The party's a much better idea," Ellen stated flatly.

"They're both good ideas," Julie said. "Why don't I tell Mr. Bowman about them and see what he thinks?"

As soon as Julie left them, Jessica turned to Elizabeth. "Are there any famous books about twins? Maybe we could dress up like them!"

Elizabeth shrugged. "I can't think of any," she said. She couldn't believe that Jessica was acting as if the decision had already been made. Elizabeth thought the VCR was a much better idea. And she had a pretty good feeling Mr. Bowman would think so, too.

Two

◇

A visit to the Carson stables always put Elizabeth in a great mood. She loved horses and went riding whenever she had a chance. Trotting along the field on a horse, with the wind in her hair, was the best feeling in the world. Some day, she vowed, she'd have a horse of her own. But for now, a handsome stallion would do nicely.

When her lesson was over, Elizabeth reluctantly climbed off the horse and gave him one last pat before the stablehand led him away. The instructor that day was Donna, who had ridden in dozens of shows. Donna had watched her carefully throughout her lesson, and when Elizabeth approached her now, she was smiling with approval.

"That was excellent, Elizabeth! You've really improved. I'm glad to see you're not holding the reins so tightly anymore."

Elizabeth basked in the instructor's praise. Donna didn't often give out compliments. "Thanks, Donna," she said gratefully.

"You're developing real form," Donna continued. "You know, Elizabeth, I think you've got the makings of a real horsewoman."

Elizabeth felt as if she'd fly all the way home. Watching for her mother's car at the stable entrance, she couldn't wait to tell her what Donna had said.

When her mother pulled up, Elizabeth ran to the car and grinned happily.

"Well, I can see you've had a good ride," Mrs. Wakefield said when Elizabeth got into the car.

"It was great, Mom! Donna says I'm becoming a real horsewoman."

"That's wonderful," Mrs. Wakefield exclaimed.

All the way home Elizabeth daydreamed about riding a magnificent mare at a big horse show and winning the blue ribbon.

As soon as the car pulled into the driveway of the Wakefields' split-level ranch, Elizabeth jumped out and ran ahead to the door. She couldn't wait to tell Jessica what Donna had said.

"Where's the fire?" asked Steven, the twins' fourteen-year-old brother. He was passing through the living room, armed with a gigantic sandwich and a soda. A bag of chips was tucked under one arm.

"Donna told me I looked really good on my horse today," Elizabeth announced proudly.

Steven didn't look the least bit impressed. "It must be nice, spending the afternoon on a horse. If you had as much homework as I have, you wouldn't have the time to—to horse around like that." He laughed at his own weak joke.

Elizabeth ignored his sarcastic tone. Steven was a freshman at Sweet Valley High, and despite his homework, he always seemed to find enough time for basketball and cleaning out the refrigerator.

"Where's Jessica?" she asked.

His mouth full, Steven nodded in the direction of the bedrooms. Elizabeth ran upstairs and headed straight for her sister's room. But just as she burst into the pink-and-white bedroom, she came to a sudden stop.

Jessica wasn't alone. Lila and Ellen were sitting on her bed, and the two of them didn't look at all pleased to see Elizabeth.

But Jessica grinned. "Lizzie, I just had the most super idea! I'm going to be Scarlett O'Hara!"

Elizabeth looked at her blankly. "Huh?"

"For the party, dummy!" Jessica said.

Elizabeth still didn't have any idea what Jessica was talking about. "What party?"

Jessica looked exasperated. "The costume party we're going to have with the money from the book fair! I'm going to go as Scarlett O'Hara, from *Gone with the Wind*." Her eyes went dreamy. "I'll wear a long hoop skirt, with lots of lace and ribbons. And I'll go to the hairdresser and have my hair done in curls."

"Tied back with a satin ribbon," Ellen suggested, and Jessica nodded happily.

"I still can't decide who I'm going to be," Lila said. "Maybe I could go as one of the girls in *Little Women*. The pretty one."

"Her name was Amy," Elizabeth murmured. Then she frowned. "Wait a minute. You don't even know if we're going to be having a party. Julie's going to ask Mr. Bowman what he thinks we should do with the money."

"Oh, Elizabeth," Lila said in disgust. "You're not still thinking we should get a VCR for the library, are you?"

"That's a stupid idea," Ellen muttered.

"It's not a stupid idea," Elizabeth said hotly. She was about to say that she thought a costume party was a stupid idea, but she held it back. After all, she shouldn't be rude to Jessica's guests.

Instead, she turned to Jessica. "When did you read *Gone with the Wind*?" She had seen the book on her parents' shelves and knew it was very thick. She couldn't imagine Jessica getting all the way through it.

Jessica shrugged. "I didn't read it. I saw the movie at Lila's last week."

"It was so great," Ellen chimed in. "Didn't you

love the part when she met Rhett Butler at the party?"

Suddenly all three of them were talking about their favorite scenes from the movie. But Elizabeth had no more time for chatter so she excused herself. Nobody even seemed to hear her when she backed out the door and went to her own room.

Unlike Jessica's room, which was always a mess, Elizabeth's bedroom was always neat. Elizabeth caught a glimpse of herself in the mirror over her dresser. She was still in her riding clothes, but no one had asked her how her lesson had gone. She hadn't even been able to tell Jessica about Donna's praise.

Feeling a little sorry for herself, Elizabeth went over to the window and looked out. Then she brightened. Amy and Julie were coming up the driveway.

She scrambled downstairs and reached the door before they had a chance to knock. "Come on in," she said, happy to have company of her own. Amy and Julie followed her back up to her bedroom.

"You must have gone riding today," Julie said.

Elizabeth nodded. At least her two friends noticed what she was wearing. "And my riding instructor told me I'm developing good form on the horse."

"That's neat," Amy replied. "If we end up having that costume party, you could go as *National Velvet*. You know, that book about the English girl who wins the big horse race."

"The Grand National," Elizabeth said automatically. Then she realized what Amy was saying, and she looked at Julie in dismay. "You mean, Mr. Bowman said we should have the party instead of buying the VCR for the library?"

"Not exactly," Julie said. "He said both the party and the VCR were good ideas, and he'd approve either of them."

Elizabeth thought about this. "I don't get it. How do we choose? Are we going to vote on it?"

"Sort of," Julie replied. "Mr. Bowman thought that we should let the class president decide."

Now Elizabeth understood. "And since we have to elect a new class president . . ."

"The book fair money could be part of the campaign," Amy finished. "Like, a person who's nominated could say, 'If I win we'll spend the money on a party.' And another candidate could say the money will go for a VCR if she's elected."

"Or he," Julie said.

"I think the class president should be a girl," Amy stated firmly. "After all, the last sixth-grade president was a girl. We shouldn't break the tradition."

Elizabeth looked thoughtful. "So the class won't just be voting on who's going to be class president, they'll also be voting on what to do with the book fair money."

"Exactly," Julie said.

"Well, I'm definitely voting for the candidate who supports the VCR idea," Amy said.

"If there is one," Julie reminded her. "Remember what Lila said at lunch today? She's dead set on getting a Unicorn as class president. And you know a Unicorn will support the party idea."

"Which do you think the sixth grade would like better?" Elizabeth asked. "The party or the VCR?"

"I think it could go either way," Julie said.

"A lot will depend on how popular the candidates are," Julie said.

Elizabeth sighed. "Then a Unicorn would probably get a lot of votes. Most of them are pretty popular. And whoever she is, she'll have the Boosters cheering her on."

"Not *all* the Boosters," Amy said cheerfully. Amy was a member of the cheering and baton squad—the only one who wasn't also a member of the Unicorn Club.

"What we need," Julie said, "is someone who is strong and popular. Someone who would support the plan to buy a VCR with the book fair money. Any ideas?"

The girls fell silent as they tried to come up with someone. "How about Nora Mercandy?" Elizabeth asked.

"I like Nora," Amy said. "But I don't think she's popular enough to beat a Unicorn."

"It's too bad you're already student council treasurer, Elizabeth," Julie remarked. "You would have been the best candidate I can think of."

"Could you do both?" Amy asked. "Is that allowed?"

"I don't know," Elizabeth said. Actually she knew that even if it was allowed, she wouldn't have the time to do both jobs. Of course, it wouldn't be all that terrible if she resigned, she thought to herself. She could think of at least one or two other student council members who would love to be treasurer.

The thought of being sixth-grade class president gave her a thrill of excitement—similar to the feeling she had when she daydreamed about winning a horse show.

She looked at her friends. They were still trying to come up with a suitable person.

"I wonder who the Unicorns will choose as their candidate," Amy said. "I hope it's not Lila."

"That might be what they're deciding right now," Elizabeth said. "Lila and Ellen are in Jessica's room."

"Really?" Amy's eyes sparkled. "Let's go into the bathroom and listen at the door. Maybe we'll hear who they're talking about!"

"Amy, that's eavesdropping!" Julie exclaimed.

The bathroom connected Elizabeth's and Jessica's room, and Elizabeth knew they'd be able to hear through the door. But she shook her head.

"I agree with Julie," she said. "That would be sneaky. I couldn't spy on Jessica."

"Besides, it doesn't make any difference who they choose," Julie said. "We should be concentrating on who our candidate's going to be. The assembly's the day after tomorrow."

Amy looked at the clock by Elizabeth's bed. "Gosh! I've got to get home."

"Me, too," Julie added.

Elizabeth walked her friends downstairs. They were all standing by the door when Jessica came down, followed by Lila and Ellen.

The girls all mumbled hello to one another, but nobody looked comfortable. Elizabeth thought it was strange that she and her sister had friends who were so different. But then, she and Jessica were very different, too.

Finally, when everyone had left, Jessica turned to Elizabeth. "Lizzie, you never told me what you think about my Scarlett O'Hara idea. Don't you think it would be a great costume for the party?"

If we have the party, Elizabeth thought. But she didn't want to get into an argument with her sister. "I guess it's a good idea. I've never read the book or seen the movie, so it's hard to say."

"We should rent a copy of the video this weekend," Jessica said enthusiastically. "You'd love it! And I'm dying to see it again, anyway."

"That would be fun," Elizabeth agreed. "Oh, Jessica, I forgot to tell you what my riding instructor said this afternoon." Quickly, she reported the compliment Donna had given her.

"That's super!" Jessica exclaimed. "Just think, Lizzie. Someday I'll be a great ballet dancer, and you'll be a great horseback rider. And we'll both be famous!"

"Girls," Mrs. Wakefield called from the kitchen. "How about setting the table for dinner?"

"OK," the twins chorused.

Together they headed for the kitchen to gather the plates and silverware. As they placed them around the table, Elizabeth thought about Amy's suggestion that they listen at the door to Jessica's room. Elizabeth knew she would never be able to do anything like that to her sister. Just as she knew Jessica would never be able to do anything intentionally mean to her.

Three

"Have you thought of anyone to nominate?" Elizabeth asked Amy as they filed into the school auditorium. The room was noisy as the entire sixth grade gathered in the front rows, and Elizabeth could barely hear her own voice.

"Maybe," Amy said, smiling mischievously. Then her expression became serious. "You know, Elizabeth, I still feel bad about supporting Peter De-Haven instead of you when you were both running for student council treasurer."

A few months earlier Amy had been Elizabeth's campaign manager in the student council elections. But a few weeks before the voting, the two girls had had an argument and Amy had switched her support to Elizabeth's opponent. Elizabeth was still able to win the race, and she and Amy had made up.

"Don't worry about that," Elizabeth said now, sitting down. "I've forgotten all about it."

Julie dashed down the aisle and took the seat on the other side of Elizabeth just as Mr. Bowman, the sixth-grade English teacher, began to climb the steps to the stage. The students settled down and the room became quiet.

Mr. Bowman supervised the *Sweet Valley Sixers*, the newspaper Elizabeth started for the sixth grade. Elizabeth thought he was a really good teacher, but that he dressed terribly. Today he was wearing a horrible striped jacket.

She twisted around in her seat to see if she could get a glimpse of her sister. Jessica wasn't hard to spot. She was sitting with the rest of the sixth-grade Unicorns. All the Unicorns wore something purple every day—it was their official color. Today Jessica had a purple scarf tied loosely around her neck. Elizabeth tried to catch her eye, but Jessica seemed to be in an intense conversation with Lila.

"Good morning, sixth graders," Mr. Bowman began. "As you all probably know by now, your class president, Linda Lloyd, has moved away from Sweet Valley. This means you'll have to elect a new class president, and you're here today to nominate your candidates. The candidates will have a little over a week to campaign, and then we will have another assembly for the actual election."

The room buzzed with excited chatter, and Mr. Bowman had to hold up his hand to get everyone's attention again.

"Now, I want you all to keep in mind that this is a very important election. The class president will be making decisions that affect all of you. So don't nominate your friends just because you like them. Nominate people who have real leadership qualities, classmates whom you trust and who will have the best interests of the sixth grade at heart. Remember—this is not a popularity contest."

A couple of kids in the audience tittered, and Mr. Bowman frowned. Elizabeth wasn't surprised to hear the giggling. Everyone knew that elections like these were *always* popularity contests, no matter what the teachers said.

Mr. Bowman walked over to a free-standing blackboard on the stage and picked up a piece of chalk. "I'll now start taking nominations," he announced.

For a second the room was silent. Then Amy leaped from her seat. "I'd like to nominate Elizabeth Wakefield."

Elizabeth's mouth fell open. She couldn't believe it! For a second she froze. Then she felt a tingle go up her spine as an approving buzz went through the room. She could feel a smile growing on her face.

"Thanks, Amy," she whispered.

"Will anyone second that nomination?" Mr. Bowman asked.

"I second it," Julie called out.

Mr. Bowman wrote ELIZABETH WAKEFIELD on the blackboard in big capital letters. Elizabeth stared at her name in awe. It was really happening—she actually had a chance to become president of the whole sixth grade!

"Now we're sure to get the VCR for the library," Amy whispered.

"Let's wait and see who else gets nominated," Elizabeth whispered back.

Mr. Bowman tapped the chalk against the blackboard. "More nominations?"

Lila got to her feet. "I have a nomination to make. . . ." she said, and paused dramatically.

"Well, who is it?" Mr. Bowman asked.

Here goes, Elizabeth thought.

"I'd like to nominate Jessica Wakefield."

Another murmur went through the room.

Elizabeth fell back in her seat. She couldn't believe what she had just heard. How could she possibly compete against her own twin sister?

"Is there a second?" Mr. Bowman asked.

From the Unicorns came a chorus of "I will."

"This is awful," Amy hissed. "What are you going to do?"

Elizabeth shook her head as she watched Mr. Bowman write JESSICA WAKEFIELD on the blackboard under her own name. What *could* she do? Jessica had never said anything about being a class officer. What was going on?

"The floor is still open for nominations," Mr. Bowman announced, raising his voice over the audience chatter. "Are there any more?"

Jim Sturbridge stood up. His mouth was twitching, as if he were trying not to burst out laughing. "Uh, yeah, I think we need a guy's name up there."

"Do you have any particular guy in mind?" Mr. Bowman asked.

The boys sitting around Jim were nudging one another and grinning. "Yeah," Jim said. "I want to nominate Randy Mason."

A giggle went through the auditorium. Elizabeth forgot about her own confusion for a moment and frowned at Jim. How could he be so mean?

She spotted Randy Mason in the back of the auditorium. Elizabeth expected to see him dying of embarrassment, his face red. Instead, he actually looked pleased. *Poor Randy,* Elizabeth thought. *He thinks he's actually got a chance. He doesn't know that this is Jim's idea of a big joke.*

There were no more nominations. Mr. Bowman dismissed them, and everyone got up. Elizabeth immediately found herself surrounded by friends.

"Congratulations!" exclaimed Sophia Rizzo.

"This is so neat!" Nora Mercandy exclaimed. "You'd be a great class president, Elizabeth!"

No one mentioned the fact that Jessica was running, too. Elizabeth assumed they thought she was upset about it. Or maybe they figured it was something she and Jessica had planned all along—like a contest.

"We have to start planning your campaign right away," Julie said happily.

Elizabeth tried to share their enthusiasm. But just hearing the word campaign made her feel strange. After all, campaigning for herself would mean campaigning against her sister!

As they moved out of the auditorium, Mr. Bowman stopped her. "Congratulations, Elizabeth," he said. "So you'll be running against your own sister! This should be an unusual experience."

Unusual wasn't the word for it, Elizabeth thought. She couldn't even think of a word that would describe the way she was feeling. She wondered if Jessica was feeling as odd about all this as she was.

After school, Jessica was waiting for Elizabeth on the front steps. "Lizzie, isn't this amazing?" she exclaimed. "We're both running for class president!"

Elizabeth smiled weakly. "Doesn't it feel a little weird to you?"

Jessica shook her head. "Not really. I think it will be fun! We'll find out who's got the most friends!"

"Don't forget about Randy Mason," Elizabeth reminded her.

Jessica rolled her eyes. "Oh, Lizzie, nobody's going to vote for him. Except for maybe a few other nerds."

As they walked home, Jessica went on and on about how thrilled she was to be running. "I was really surprised when Lila said she thought I'd be the best candidate. She thinks I'm one of the most popular Unicorns, so I have the best chance of winning."

"But do you really want to be class president?" Elizabeth asked. "It's a lot of work."

Jessica shrugged. "I can always get the other Unicorns to help me."

Elizabeth looked at her sister seriously. "Jessica, I don't want this election to come between us. No matter what happens, I don't want us to start fighting, or anything like that."

Jessica laughed. "We're already fighting, in a way. That's just what happens when two people want the same thing and only one of them can have it."

"But it's going to be a fair fight, right?" Elizabeth asked hopefully.

"Oh, sure," Jessica said in an offhand way. Her eyes were sparkling. "And when I win we can have a fabulous costume party."

Elizabeth stared at her twin. Jessica was talking as if she were sure she'd be elected. "What do you mean, *when* you win? You mean, *if* you win."

Jessica gave a little laugh. "Face it, Lizzie. With the Unicorns behind me, my chances are better than yours. Lila's already making terrific plans for my campaign. You know I'm going to end up winning."

Elizabeth had a suspicion that Jessica might be right. But she didn't have to be so confident!

"Don't be so sure of yourself," Elizabeth said, trying to keep from getting angry. "I'm sure Amy and Julie and I are going to come up with a pretty good campaign, too."

"Of course you will," Jessica said. "I just hope you're not too disappointed when you lose."

"Jessica!" Elizabeth exclaimed. "Stop it! I've got just as good a chance at winning as you do, and you know it."

"I do?" Jessica asked impishly.

Elizabeth sighed deeply. She should know better than to argue with Jessica when she was feeling so confident. But she was determined not to let Jessica goad her into an argument. Running against her sister for president was hard enough without having it get nasty. She'd let Jessica say anything she wanted.

But Elizabeth was confident that she—not Jessica—was going to win.

At dinner that night Jessica announced the news to the family. "Elizabeth and I are both candidates for sixth-grade class president!"

"Congratulations!" Mrs. Wakefield exclaimed.

"That's wonderful, girls!" Mr. Wakefield said proudly.

Steven's response was a little different. "You're kidding! You guys are running against each other?" He whistled. "Better watch out for World War Three!"

"Don't talk like that, Steven," Mrs. Wakefield scolded. "Elizabeth and Jessica are running *for* something, not *against* each other."

"That's right," Mr. Wakefield agreed. "Elizabeth and Jessica would never let anything like this come between them. Would you, girls?"

Elizabeth shook her head vigorously.

"Of course not, Dad," Jessica said, her voice sounding sugary sweet.

Mr. Wakefield nodded in approval. "I expect both of you to have a healthy and friendly competition. No back-stabbing or anything like that. And whichever twin wins, I'm sure the other will be happy for her."

"There's someone else running, too," Elizabeth said. "A boy named Randy Mason."

"We don't have to worry about Randy Mason, though," Jessica said confidently. "Nobody's going to vote for him."

Mr. Wakefield frowned. "You sound pretty sure of yourself, Jessica. But remember: never underestimate your competition."

"And don't count your chickens before they're hatched," their mother added.

"And if the two of you need a referee, just let me know," Steven offered, grinning.

Later that evening, as she was finishing her homework, Elizabeth's thoughts drifted to the campaign. She tried to push her worries out of her head.

So what if Jessica was acting like she was absolutely positive she would win? She had a good chance, too.

But that wasn't really what was worrying her. It was the campaign. She knew how mean Lila could be—and if Lila was handling Jessica's campaign, there was no telling what could go on.

Don't be ridiculous, she told herself sternly. Jessica would never do anything sneaky or nasty to win—not to her own sister. It would be just like their father said: a healthy competition. If Elizabeth won, Jessica would be happy for her. And if Jessica won, Elizabeth knew she'd feel the same. A little thing like being sixth-grade class president couldn't possibly tear two sisters apart.

Feeling better, Elizabeth decided it was time for a snack. She piled her books and notebooks neatly on her desk and went downstairs.

Even before she entered the kitchen she could hear Jessica's voice.

"Really, Steven, if you were a sixth grader, wouldn't you rather spend the book fair money on a fantastic costume party than on a dumb VCR?"

"What's going on?" Elizabeth asked, standing in the entrance with her hands on her hips.

Jessica looked smug. "I'm just trying out my presidential platform on Steven."

"Well, how about this?" Elizabeth turned to Steven. "Wouldn't you rather have a president who has more important things on her mind than costume parties?"

Steven looked from one to the other. "Hmm," he murmured, his expression very serious. "I'm going to have to think about this before I make my decision. I want to know exactly what you're willing to do for my vote."

"How about homemade peanut chocolate-chip cookies?" Jessica asked.

Steven cocked his head to one side and considered this. "That's not bad. Okay, Lizzie, what are you offering to top that?"

Elizabeth rolled her eyes. "Jess, he's not in the sixth grade, remember? He doesn't even *have* a vote."

Jessica reddened. "Oh, yeah. That's right." Then she started giggling. "Forget the cookies, Steven."

At the sight of her brother's disappointed face, Elizabeth had to laugh, too.

Four

◇

Early Saturday afternoon Elizabeth stood in the doorway to Jessica's bedroom. She couldn't believe what she was seeing.

Jessica Wakefield was cleaning up her room.

"What—what's going on?" Elizabeth managed to ask. Jessica's room was always a mess. But now Jessica was on her hands and knees, pulling some knee socks out from under her bed. She glanced at Elizabeth briefly.

"I'm cleaning up."

"I can see that," Elizabeth said. "How come? What's the big occasion?"

Jessica scrambled to her feet and dropped the socks into her laundry basket. "Some of the Unicorns are coming over this afternoon. We're going to start working on my campaign plans."

"Why don't you meet in the living room?" Elizabeth asked. "There's more space."

Jessica smiled secretively. "We'd rather work in my bedroom, where I can close the door."

It didn't take long for Elizabeth to realize what Jessica meant. "Jess, you don't have to worry about me listening to your plans. I'm not interested in stealing your ideas."

Jessica didn't look convinced. "Oh, really?"

"Besides," Elizabeth continued, "I'm not even going to be home this afternoon. Amy and Julie and I are going to meet at Casey's Place." She grinned mischievously. "We're going to be working on *my* campaign."

"See?" Jessica said triumphantly. "You don't want me to know your plans any more than I want you to know mine! That's why you and your friends aren't working here at home."

"That's not true," Elizabeth shot back. "It's just that we can get hot fudge sundaes at Casey's Place, and we can't at home."

Jessica pulled the bedspread over her bed without even bothering to straighten the wrinkles on the sheets underneath. "I'm not blaming you, Lizzie. If you really want to win an election, you do what you have to do."

"Like what?"

"Well, you work up a good campaign plan, and

you don't let the other side know what you're doing. That's what politics is all about."

Elizabeth looked at her sister skeptically. "Since when do you know anything about politics?"

"Since I became a politician!" With that, Jessica did a pirouette.

"Now you're the world's first political balle-rina," Elizabeth declared.

Jessica giggled. "Maybe I should do a dance when I give my campaign speech." She executed a series of perfect turns while saying, "Vote for me."

Her performance made Elizabeth start giggling, too. "Maybe I should give my speech on horseback."

"I can see it now!" Jessica cried. "You, riding up to the auditorium stage at Sweet Valley Middle School on horseback!"

The image made both sisters laugh. By the time she left home, Elizabeth felt pretty good about the whole situation. Jessica might be determined to win the election, but at least they could still joke about it.

Casey's Place was at the Valley Mall, and it was the most popular ice cream parlor in town. When Elizabeth entered with Amy and Julie, the place was noisy and crowded. There was only one empty booth, and they settled down in it.

"It's good we're getting started right away," Eliz-abeth told her friends. "Jessica's got a bunch of Uni-corns coming over today to work on her campaign."

Julie looked worried. "I hope Lila isn't planning

any dirty tricks to play on you." Lila was famous for her clever schemes.

Elizabeth shook her head firmly. "Even if she does, Jessica would never go along with it. She wouldn't do anything like that."

Just then a waitress came over to their table. "What can I get you girls?"

Elizabeth knew exactly what she wanted. "A hot fudge sundae, please. With vanilla ice cream."

"Same for me, please," Julie said.

Amy was having more trouble deciding. "I'll have a strawberry—no, a butter pecan—no, wait. I want a banana split with cherry-vanilla ice cream and butterscotch sauce."

The waitress looked horrified, but Amy just leaned back in her seat, happy with her selection.

As soon as the waitress left them, Julie leaned forward and spoke to Elizabeth in a serious voice. "I know you don't think Jessica would go along with one of Lila's plans. But let's face it, Elizabeth— Jessica's been willing to go along with some pretty nasty schemes before."

Elizabeth had to admit Julie was right. She remembered some tricks Jessica had pulled off—on chubby, unpopular Lois Waller, and on Nora Mercandy, making everyone think her grandmother was a witch.

"That's true," she said slowly. "But I'm her sister. She'd never do anything like that to me."

Amy peered around the side of the booth.

"What are you doing?" Elizabeth asked.

"Shh, I think that's Randy Mason in the next booth," Amy whispered.

Elizabeth looked at her disapprovingly. "Don't spy on them, Amy!"

But the girls couldn't help overhearing part of the conversation going on behind them.

"We're so proud of you, Randy!" a woman's voice proclaimed.

"My son, the president," boomed a male voice.

"I don't know if I can win, Dad," the girls heard Randy say, "but I'm going to do my best. I think I've got some good ideas, and if I can get the other kids to listen to them, I just might have a real chance to win."

Suddenly Elizabeth felt embarrassed about listening to them. She quickly turned to the others.

"Let's talk about the campaign."

Julie pulled out a notebook and a pen. "I know the book fair money is what's on everybody's mind. But I think we should come up with some other ideas, too." Her tone became businesslike. "Now, Elizabeth, if you're elected class president, what would you do for the sixth grade?"

Just then their ice cream arrived, and everyone started to eat. As she licked hot fudge off her spoon, Elizabeth tried to think of what she could do as president.

"I have an idea," Elizabeth said. "In the high school they give an award every year for the best teacher. How about starting an award for the best teacher in the sixth grade? We could vote on it at the end of the year."

"Yeah," Amy said enthusiastically. "And maybe we could collect money for a trophy to give the teacher."

"Best teacher award," Julie said aloud as she wrote that down.

"How about the food in the cafeteria?" Amy asked. "Everyone's always complaining about that. Why don't you say that if you're elected, there will be better lunches?"

Elizabeth frowned. "I don't know if I can do anything about that."

Julie wrote it down anyway.

"Don't forget the VCR," Amy said. "I still think the book fair money is gong to be the biggest issue."

Julie nodded, and at the bottom of the list she wrote, *VCR for library*.

"This is good," Julie said, looking at her list with approval. "I bet all Jessica will say is 'more parties.' This will show that Elizabeth is a much more serious candidate."

"You know," Amy said thoughtfully, "my father told me that some politicians win their elections by showing how bad the other candidate is."

Elizabeth shook her head firmly. "No. I could never say anything bad about Jessica. Not in public, at least."

"Hello, Elizabeth."

Elizabeth turned and saw Randy Mason standing by their booth. "Hi, Randy."

"I just wanted to congratulate you on your nomination," Randy said politely.

"Uh, thanks," Elizabeth said. "Congratulations
to you, too."

Randy beamed. "I must say, I was pretty surprised to be nominated."

Elizabeth felt miserable. If only Randy knew
how everyone was laughing at the idea of him running for class president. She forced herself to smile.
"Good luck!"

"Same to you," he said. "'Bye."

As they watched him walk away, Amy whispered, "Why does everyone think he's such a nerd?
He seems kind of nice."

"Who knows?" Elizabeth sighed. "Look, about
these campaign promises—how am I going to let all
the kids know about them? I can't talk to everyone in
the sixth grade in one week."

"You can make a flyer," Julie suggested. "Put all
these ideas down neatly on a ditto master. Then
we'll run it off on the machine in the library Monday
morning."

"We can hand them out in the cafeteria during
lunch," Amy added. "And we can wait by the exits
after school and hand them out there, too."

"OK!" Elizabeth was starting to feel excited.

"These are great ideas," Julie said, looking over

the list with approval. "I bet the other kids will think so, too."

They had long since finished their ice cream, and Elizabeth noticed the waitress looking at them. There were people at the entrance waiting for tables to empty.

"I guess we'd better get going," she said.

"I'll go call my mother to come get us," Amy said. She walked toward the pay phone.

"Hey, there's Tom McKay and Ken Matthews," Julie said. Tom and Ken were both in the sixth grade.

"Let's try out your ideas on them," Julie suggested. She waved to the boys, and they came over.

"You know Elizabeth's running for class president," Julie said, holding out the list. "What do you think of her plans?"

The boys didn't look particularly impressed until they saw the part about better food in the cafeteria. "Hey, if you can do that, you've got my vote," Tom said.

Elizabeth bit her lower lip and smiled apologetically. "I'm not really sure I can do anything about that—" she began.

But Ken interrupted. "A VCR! That's a great idea! The basketball coach said if we had a VCR at school, he'd tape some pro games for us. It would really help the team."

"See!" Julie said happily to Elizabeth. "I told you everyone would like your ideas." She turned to the boys. "You know, Jessica's running, too, and she wants to spend the book fair money on a costume party instead of a VCR."

The boys looked at each other. "A costume party would be fun," Tom said, and Ken nodded.

Julie's face fell. "Well, think about which you'd rather have," she murmured.

"OK," the boys said in unison, and walked away.

Amy came back to the table. "My mother's on her way. And I've got some news. She said Lila just called me."

"What was Lila calling *you* about?" Elizabeth asked.

"She says the Boosters are having a pool party at her place next week. She's inviting a whole bunch of sixth graders to get them to support Jessica."

"A pool party," Elizabeth said in dismay. "The kids will love that, especially after a full day of classes. And if the Boosters are organizing it, it will be a pretty terrific party."

"Well, I'm not going," Amy said staunchly. "The only reason Lila invited me is because I'm a Booster. She knows I'm supporting you."

"And just because kids go to the party doesn't mean they'll vote for Jessica," Julie added.

The girls got up to leave. "Your parents must be pretty happy," Amy said. "No matter what happens, a Wakefield is going to win."

"That's true," Elizabeth said. But for some reason, she couldn't get Randy Mason out of her mind.

As she entered the house, Elizabeth wondered if the Unicorns were still upstairs working on Jessica's campaign. She didn't hear any noise, so she walked into the living room.

Steven was at the television, flipping the channels. On top of the set sat a plate holding a gigantic slice of cake.

"If you're looking for your archenemy," he said, "she went out with her friends."

Elizabeth didn't bother to respond. She just went up to her room. After sitting down at her desk, she pulled out a sheet of paper and picked up a black felt-tip pen.

Vote for Elizabeth Wakefield, she wrote on top. Under that, very neatly, she printed:

VCR for Library
Best Teacher Award
Better Cafeteria Food

She paused after the last one. Could she really promise that? It would probably help get her elected. But unless she was prepared to make lunches every day for the entire sixth grade, she couldn't guarantee it.

Sighing, she crumpled up the paper and started

again. She listed as many promises as she could think of, and under those, in larger letters and all capitals, she wrote: VCR FOR THE LIBRARY.

She held the paper up to admire her work.

"What are you doing?" came Jessica's voice from the doorway.

"I'm working on a flyer for my campaign," she said. Jessica sauntered over to get a closer look.

"Big deal," she said. "Nobody cares about a best teacher award. And who's going to read a dumb flyer anyway?"

Elizabeth drew herself up and eyed Jessica squarely. "It's better than a stupid pool party at Lila's."

Jessica's eyebrows shot up. "How did you find out about that?"

"None of your business," Elizabeth said.

Jessica's eyes darkened so deeply, they almost looked navy blue. "So, you're already spying on my campaign!"

"I wasn't spying!" Elizabeth replied hotly.

"Well, it sounds like that to me," Jessica said in a haughty voice. She whirled around and headed for the door. When she reached it, she looked back over her shoulder.

"Two can play this game, you know," she declared. Then she walked out.

Elizabeth stared after her in bewilderment. What was *that* supposed to mean?

In the pit of her stomach she had a funny feeling that she'd soon find out.

Five

◇

Clutching a folder in her hand, Elizabeth walked into the library media center a half hour before homeroom. The room was almost empty.

Elizabeth hurried over to the ditto machine, where Julie was waiting for her.

"Let me see how it looks," Julie said. Carefully Elizabeth opened the folder to reveal her flyer.

"Excellent," Julie declared. "It looks really professional. Too bad we don't have time to take it to a real printer. Then we could have put your picture on it, too."

Elizabeth laughed. "Maybe that's not such a great idea. Someone might think it's a flyer for Jessica."

"Good point," Julie said. "How many do you think we should run off?"

"Enough for the whole class and some extras. I guess that would be about a hundred fifty."

Julie set the counter and positioned the ditto master in place.

"Here goes," she said, and hit the button. The pages had just started printing when Amy came in, breathless, her stringy blond hair falling into her eyes.

"Sorry I'm late," she apologized. "How do they look?" She grabbed one of the sheets as it came out of the chute. "Great! But how come you didn't put down 'better cafeteria food'?"

"I decided I'd better not make promises I might not be able to keep."

Ms. Luster, the librarian, came over to them. "What are you girls up to?" she asked, smiling.

"Elizabeth's running for sixth-grade class president," Amy told her.

"We're running off flyers to hand out," Elizabeth said, and showed one to the librarian.

Ms. Luster's eyes widened as she read Elizabeth's campaign promises. "A VCR for the library!" she exclaimed. "We could certainly use one. But where are you going to get the money for it?"

"The profits from the book fair," Elizabeth replied. "The sixth grade's running it, and the class president gets to decide what to do with the money."

Ms. Luster beamed at her. "Well, this is impressive! I wish I had a vote."

"I think we've got enough here," Julie said, lifting the stack of flyers off the machine.

"Good luck," Ms. Luster said. "Now I've got to get back to work. I've got three boxes of new books to unpack."

Elizabeth's eyes lit up. "New books? Do you need any help?"

"I suppose I could use a few extra pairs of hands," Ms. Luster said.

Julie put the flyers down on the table, and the three girls followed the librarian to her office.

"I love the smell of new books," Elizabeth said as she pulled open a box. "I hope there are some new horse stories."

"Ooh, this looks good!" Julie said enthusiastically, holding up a music book. Julie's parents were both musicians, and Julie had taken piano lessons since she was six. "Can I check this one out?"

"I have to stamp it first, and put a card pocket in it," Ms. Luster told her. "But I promise you'll be the first to get it when it's ready to go out."

"Wow!" Amy exclaimed, flipping through a book. "*Women in Sports*! This one's mine!"

The girls soon got the boxes unpacked and arranged them on a book truck. Elizabeth glanced at the clock. "We've got ten minutes until the bell rings. Maybe we should go stand by the front door and hand out some of the flyers."

"Thanks for your help," Ms. Luster called out to them as they left the office.

The girls went back to the table where Julie had left the flyers. But the flyers weren't there. Even the ditto master was gone.

"I'm sure this is where I left them," Julie said, frowning. Quickly, the girls searched the other tables. There were no flyers anywhere.

"Excuse me," Elizabeth said to an older girl who was reading at a table. "Did you see a stack of paper on that table?"

The girl raised her eyes from the book only long enough to shake her head.

Not knowing what else to do, the girls looked around the floor, under chairs and behind shelves. Amy even checked behind the plants on the windowsill. But the flyers seemed to have vanished.

"What could have happened to them?" Elizabeth asked anxiously.

"Maybe somebody put books on top of them and then carried them away accidentally," Julie said hopefully.

"Maybe," Elizabeth said doubtfully. She couldn't picture someone walking off with a hundred fifty sheets of paper and not even noticing them.

"I'm sure that's what happened," Amy said cheerfully. "I'll bet whoever it was will turn them in to the Lost and Found in the principal's office."

"And let's check the bulletin board outside the cafeteria at lunch," Julie suggested.

"I just hope whoever took them doesn't throw them away," Elizabeth said. "I guess we can always make more. But this puts us a day behind on the campaign."

The bell was about to ring, and the girls took off for homeroom. All morning Elizabeth waited for someone to come up to her and give back the flyers. But nobody did, and no one she asked seemed to know anything about them.

When lunchtime came, she ran to the cafeteria, hoping to find a notice on the bulletin board telling her the flyers were found. Quickly she looked over the messages: lost gloves, found notebook, a soccer game on Friday. She didn't see anything about flyers, but another notice caught her eye.

For maximum efficiency
in advocating rights and issues
pertinent to all sixth-grade students,
vote for Randy Mason

Elizabeth read it, and then read it again. She still wasn't exactly sure what it meant.

"What do you think?" The question came from a voice behind her. Elizabeth turned around and faced a proud-looking Randy Mason.

Elizabeth had to pause a moment before replying. "It's—it's interesting," she said carefully. Then she decided she might as well be honest. After all, if she didn't understand it, most of the other kids probably wouldn't either.

"I'm not sure what it means, Randy."

His face dropped a little. "Really? I guess you're right. Some of the words are kind of, kind of—"

"Fancy," Elizabeth supplied.

Randy blushed. "I used a thesaurus to get bigger words. I thought it would look impressive."

"You know," Elizabeth said, "if you're going to tell kids what you'll do for them as class president, you ought to use words they'll understand. Otherwise, they won't know what you're talking about."

As she spoke, Elizabeth was wondering why she was bothering to help an opponent. But Randy was so sweet and pitiful, she couldn't just let him make a fool of himself. Besides, he didn't really have a chance of winning anyway.

Randy seemed to appreciate her remarks. "I suppose I should write it over. I just wish I knew what to take a stand on. I guess I don't know what the other sixth graders are talking about."

"Well, there's the book fair money," Elizabeth said.

"What about it?"

"Since the sixth grade is running the book fair, the class president gets to decide what to do with the profits. I'm telling kids that if I'm elected, we'll use the money to buy a VCR for the library."

Randy nodded in approval. "That's a good idea."

"And if Jessica wins, she wants to use the money for a costume party."

"A lot of kids would like that," Randy said. "I guess I should have an idea, too, right?"

"Right," Elizabeth said.

"Thanks a lot," Randy said gratefully, and walked off.

Later that afternoon, when Elizabeth was sitting in English class, an announcement came over the intercom.

"Elizabeth Wakefield, please come to the office after this period."

"Someone must have turned in the flyers," she whispered happily to Amy. The minute class was over, she and Amy rushed to the office.

Elizabeth greeted the secretary cheerfully, but the secretary's face was stern. She held out a wet and crumpled paper.

"Young lady, what is the meaning of this?"

Elizabeth stared in dismay at the paper. It was soggy and wrinkled, but she knew at once what it was.

"That's one of my flyers!"

"Exactly," the secretary said. "And if you wanted to throw them away, you should have used a wastebasket. *Not* the school fountain."

"What?" Elizabeth said faintly.

"There must be hundreds of these floating in

the fountain in front of this school. It's disgraceful! I wouldn't have expected you to be careless like this, Elizabeth. And as soon as school is over today, I expect you and your friends to clean them out."

Elizabeth almost said, I didn't put them there! But she was afraid to open her mouth and speak. She felt on the verge of tears, and she didn't want to burst out crying in the middle of the office.

"Yes, ma'am," she managed to say, then hurried out of the office with Amy close behind her.

"I can't believe this!" Amy exclaimed. "How did the flyers get into the school fountain?"

"I don't know," Elizabeth said. She could hear her voice quavering. "I guess it's somebody's dumb idea of a joke."

"Somebody like Jessica?"

Elizabeth scowled. "Don't be ridiculous, Amy. Jessica wouldn't do something like that to me."

For the rest of the afternoon Elizabeth felt dazed. When the last bell rang, she went outside and met Julie and Amy at the fountain. Sure enough, there were all her flyers, completely ruined.

The girls didn't say much as they began pulling the sheets out of the cold water. After gathering a bunch, they silently carried them to a trash can. They had just returned to the fountain to pull out the rest of them when Julie stopped and stared at a point behind Elizabeth.

"Look!" she exclaimed angrily.

Elizabeth turned. Just a few yards away, Lila

and Ellen were watching them. Lila had a nasty sneer on her face. When they saw Elizabeth looking at them, Ellen burst into giggles, and the two of them ran away.

"This was a Unicorn plot!" Amy cried.

"But how did they find out about the flyers?" Julie asked. "Did either of you tell anyone about them?"

"Not me," Amy said.

Elizabeth was silent for a minute. "Jessica saw the flyer in my room yesterday," she said finally.

"I hate to say this," Amy said, "but I'll bet Jessica did this. Or she got one of the other Unicorns to do it."

Elizabeth opened her mouth to argue, but then clamped it shut. Maybe Amy was right. And maybe this was what Jessica meant when she'd said, "Two can play this game."

Six

◇

Monday, late afternoon, Jessica was having the time of her life. About twenty-five kids had gathered around the pool behind Lila's huge, beautiful house. And Jessica was right where she always liked to be— at the center of attention.

It was a great party. Alongside the pool there was a grill and a buffet table, where potato salad, cole slaw, pretzels, corn chips, and lots of other things were set out. There was even a big cake, all white except for the tiny pink candy roses that encircled it, and the elaborate script on top. In pink icing it spelled out, JESSICA FOR PRESIDENT.

Jessica didn't know if the party would get her any votes, but it was definitely fun. Everyone was having a good time. Friends were either jumping into the pool or getting pushed in. She tried to stay a little distance from the water since her hair looked absolutely perfect and she didn't want to get it wet. So she just stretched out on a deck chair and let everyone come to her.

"Congratulations!" Betsy Gordon called from the other side of the pool. She had just arrived with two other seventh-grade Unicorns. Jessica flashed her biggest smile and waved to them. Of course, being seventh graders meant they couldn't vote for her, but they still might have influence.

Charlie Cashman ambled over to her. He was a sixth grader who frequently got into trouble at school with his best friend, Jerry McAllister. But they'd both helped the Unicorns out with some of their schemes, and Charlie had a vote, so Jessica gave him a big smile, too.

"This is cool," Charlie said approvingly. "Once you're sixth-grade president, we can do some really wild stuff at school."

Jessica wasn't sure what he meant. All she had in mind was that big costume party. But she nodded enthusiastically and said, "Oh, sure, absolutely," before he ran back to the pool and shoved in some girl.

Jessica turned to Janet Howell, Lila's cousin, and president of the Unicorn Club, who was sitting on the chair next to hers.

"What does a class president do, anyway?"
Janet shrugged. "I haven't the slightest idea."

"Oh."

"But it's good that you're running," Janet continued. "This will give the Unicorns more power."

Jessica nodded. "I hope it's not too much work, though. I don't want to have to start collecting canned foods, or anything like that."

Janet didn't reply. She was busy adjusting her chair so she could get the full benefit of the sun. A few yards away Lila was saying something to a group of kids, and they were all laughing. Jessica decided it was worth getting up to find out what was so funny.

"What are you guys laughing about?" she asked them.

"We pulled a great stunt on your sister today," Lila told her. "She left a bunch of flyers sitting on a table in the library. Ellen saw them in there."

Jessica had forgotten about Elizabeth's flyers. "What about them?"

Lila giggled. "Well, when Elizabeth wasn't looking, Ellen grabbed the whole stack. We dumped them in the fountain in front of school. You should have seen Elizabeth's face when she found them floating around! And then she had to fish them all out. It was a riot!"

For a moment Jessica felt a little funny. Elizabeth had worked pretty hard on those flyers. But still, this *was* a competition. And the image of those neatly printed flyers floating around the fountain was kind of funny.

"Tell us about the party we're going to have with the book fair money," Brooke Dennis said, walking over to Jessica. Brooke wasn't a Unicorn, but she was a good friend of the Wakefield twins.

The tiny bit of guilt Jessica felt about Elizabeth's flyers went out of her mind. "It's going to be super! We'll have lots of money to spend, so we can have good refreshments and real decorations. And everyone has to come dressed as their favorite character from a book." Jessica paused. Should she tell them that she was planning to go as Scarlett O'Hara? Better not, she decided—somebody might steal her idea.

Brooke smoothed her hair and frowned slightly. "Does it have to be a book character? Can't it be someone from a movie?"

Brooke's father was a famous Hollywood scriptwriter, and Brooke was more interested in movies than books. Lila seemed to agree with her.

"I think that's a good idea," she said. "Movies are made from scripts, and a script is sort of like a book."

"Would that be OK, Jessica?" Brooke asked. Jessica liked the way Brooke seemed to be asking for permission. She pretended to be considering the suggestion carefully.

"Sure," Jessica said. "Why not? After all, if I'm class president, I can make the rules any way I want them to be. OK, I'll say everyone can come as characters from books or movies." She paused, and then added, "But not from television shows."

"Why not?" one kid asked.

"Because I say so," Jessica said firmly.

Just saying that made her feel powerful and important. So this is what being sixth-grade president meant—making rules and telling everyone what they could and couldn't do! She was definitely going to enjoy the job. Even Lila seemed to be looking at her with new respect.

"You sound like you're pretty sure you're going to win," Brooke said, smiling. "Your sister's pretty popular, too, you know."

Ellen Riteman smirked. "Yeah, but she's no fun, and everyone knows that. If she were president, the sixth grade would only get to do boring, serious stuff."

Jessica knew that wasn't really true, but she didn't say anything. After all, it could only bring her more votes if everyone thought Elizabeth was boring and dull.

Kimberly Haver, a seventh-grade Unicorn, tossed her head so her thick black hair tumbled around her shoulders. "I thought about maybe running for seventh-grade president this year. But I decided not to."

"How come?" Jessica asked.

Kimberly made a face. "I didn't want to go to all those meetings."

Jessica's face fell. "Meetings?" That could definitely interfere with her social life. She shrugged. "When I'm president, maybe I'll just do away with meetings."

Later, as she waited at the grill for the cook to fix her a hot dog, Jessica thought again about Elizabeth and those flyers. Something in the back of her mind was bothering her.

Elizabeth probably didn't know for sure who had thrown her flyers into the fountain, Jessica reasoned. But her sister might think that she'd had something to do with it. And in that case, Elizabeth just might be considering getting back at her.

Jessica tried to push this disturbing thought from her mind. Elizabeth wasn't the type to think of any really nasty tricks. And what could she do anyway? Spread lies and rumors? That wasn't Elizabeth's style.

Jessica took her hot dog and sat down at the edge of the pool, dangling her feet in the water as she ate. It was a beautiful day, she was having a good time, and there was nothing to worry about. But as hard as she tried to keep them away, thoughts of Elizabeth kept coming back to her.

Lila sat down next to her. "Why are you frowning like that? You'll get wrinkles if you're not careful."

"I'm a little worried about Elizabeth," she admitted. "What if she tries to get even with me for what Ellen did?"

"She might try," Lila said. "I know *I* would. You'd better be on guard. Maybe when you get home you should try to sneak in her room and see if she's planning anything."

"That's not a bad idea," Jessica said thoughtfully.

Opening the front door to the house, Jessica heard laughter coming from the top of the stairs. And she distinctly heard, "It's a fabulous plan."

A second later Elizabeth, Julie, and Amy appeared. They stopped laughing as soon as they saw Jessica.

"What's the fabulous plan?" Jessica asked, smiling brightly.

Elizabeth and Amy exchanged secretive glances. "Oh, something for my campaign," Elizabeth murmured. "How was your party?"

Jessica's eyes darted from Julie to Amy to Elizabeth. They all had the same smug expression. Something was going on here but Jessica pretended to be unconcerned.

"Oh, it was great," she said casually.

"I'll call you later," Julie said to Elizabeth. "Then we can finish making the plans for . . . you know."

Elizabeth grinned and nodded. The second Julie and Amy were out the door, Jessica gave Elizabeth a hard look. "What's going on?"

"Nothing that concerns you," Elizabeth said.

But she looked so confident that it was driving Jessica wild.

"Hope you didn't get too wet fishing those flyers out of the fountain," she snapped.

Elizabeth glared at her. "Excuse me," she said coldly. "I'm going to help Mom with dinner." She whirled around and marched out of the room.

Jessica watched her go into the kitchen. She waited a minute, and then heard the sound of running water. That meant Elizabeth was probably washing vegetables. Quickly, Jessica ran upstairs, stopping on the landing to look back over her shoulder and make sure no one was watching. She headed directly for Elizabeth's room and pushed the door open.

The room looked normal. As usual, the bed was neatly made and everything was in its place. Feverishly, Jessica started looking around. There had to be some clue as to what Elizabeth and her friends were planning.

A search of her desk and an investigation of the closet revealed nothing. Then Jessica spotted something sticking out from under the bed. She glanced back out the door to make sure Elizabeth wasn't coming up the stairs. Then she got down on her hands and knees and pulled.

It was a big cardboard poster. On the top, in huge letters, it read, ELIZABETH WAKEFIELD FOR SIXTH-GRADE PRESIDENT. Under that, the letters were just slightly smaller: SHOW YOUR SUPPORT AT A

RALLY AFTER THE SOCCER GAME. HEAR ELIZABETH TELL WHAT SHE'LL DO AS YOUR CLASS PRESIDENT.

Jessica thought she heard steps on the stairs. She quickly pushed the poster back under the bed and hurried out of the room.

Passing the stairs, she almost bumped into Steven heading for his room. He grinned at her. "What are you doing—spying on the opposition?"

Jessica laughed nervously. "Don't be silly. I just thought I'd left a sweater in there. I was looking for it."

"Yeah, sure," Steven said. "Is it time to set up the battle stations yet?"

Jessica rolled her eyes. "It's not a battle, it's a campaign." With that, she tossed her head and went toward her room. But before she went in, she looked back at Steven.

"Uh, Steven," she said, "do me a favor, OK? Don't tell Elizabeth I was in her room."

Steven looked at her knowingly. "If I don't, what's in it for me?"

Jessica thought rapidly. "I'll do the dishes for you next time it's your turn."

Steven considered this. "How about the next two times?"

Jessica sighed. "OK." Then she went to her room, sat on her bed, and thought.

So that was it—Elizabeth was planning a rally. Everyone was planning to go to the soccer game on Friday, and kids would probably hang around afterward. It was the perfect time to get the attention of the entire sixth grade.

She wished she'd thought of a rally first. What could she possibly do to top it? Jessica heard her mother call from downstairs to set the table.

"I'll be right down," she shouted. She had to think of something—and she knew she needed help, so she ran straight to the telephone.

"Lila, it's me," she said a few seconds later. "I found out that Elizabeth's planning something." After describing the poster she'd found she continued with, "Elizabeth's a good talker, and she'll have all those kids there already. She just might be able to convince them to vote for her."

"That's true," Lila admitted. "This is definitely not good for us."

"I'm trying to think of something we can do to top it," Jessica said.

For a second there was silence on the other end. Then Lila's voice came over, cool and confident. "We don't have to *top* it. We just have to *stop* it."

Jessica almost gasped. Sabotage an entire rally? "How are we going to do it?"

"Don't worry," Lila said. "I'll think of something. We have four whole days to plan something."

As she hung up, Jessica had a moment of doubt. Could she really go along with a plot to ruin her sister's rally? Then an image of the crowd at Friday's soccer game came into her mind, and her heart hardened.

No way was Elizabeth going to have a big rally with a huge audience cheering for her. No way.

Seven

◇

Waiting in the school parking lot, Jessica could hear a roar coming from the field where the soccer game was going on.

"It sounds like we scored," said Lila.

"Yeah," Jessica agreed, but her mind wasn't on the game. She had other things to think about. She checked her watch. "Are you sure they're going to get here before the game's over?"

Lila didn't look the least bit anxious. "They'll be here," she assured Jessica. "My father said they'd be delivered this afternoon and he'd have them sent directly here by special messenger."

Jessica looked at her watch again. The game would probably be over in about fifteen minutes.

She wished she could feel as confident as Lila looked.

For the past few days, every time she'd passed Elizabeth's poster, she'd had to clamp her mouth shut to keep from telling people her plan. The sign announcing Elizabeth's rally after the soccer game had been hanging right next to the bulletin board outside the cafeteria, and Jessica had seen a lot of kids looking at it.

Right now she could picture Elizabeth sitting in the stands, nervous and excited about giving a campaign speech in front of all those people. Well, Elizabeth had nothing to be nervous about, Jessica thought. Her sister didn't know that by the time she was ready to give her silly little speech, there'd be nobody there to hear it.

"Here they come now," Lila announced. A big black car with SPEEDY MESSENGER SERVICE written on its door drove into the parking lot. The girls ran over to it as it pulled up next to the curb.

A man in a uniform got out. "Miss Lila Fowler?" he inquired.

"Yes," Lila replied importantly. "Put the boxes right over here."

The man opened the trunk of the car and began hoisting big cardboard boxes onto the sidewalk. Each carton was emblazoned with the name of a record company.

As soon as he put the first one down, Jessica quickly ripped it open. She gazed in awe at the stack of records, neatly encased in paper jackets. She carefully lifted one out and examined the label.

"Johnny Buck's new single! And it's not even in the record stores yet!"

She and Lila rapidly opened the other boxes and checked to make sure they were all the same.

"I can't believe your father was able to get all these for us!" Jessica exclaimed.

"He's got business contacts at the record company," Lila told her. "All he had to do was make a few calls."

"Just wait till everyone finds out we're giving these away free, right here," Jessica said gleefully. Who'd want to stick around for Elizabeth's rally?"

Lila nodded. "I've told all the Unicorns to go through the stands and spread the word. And they're telling everyone there's not enough to go around, so if they want a free record, they'd better be here the second the game is finished. They'll probably start coming even before the game's over."

Jessica's eyes shone. She knew Lila was right. Johnny Buck was a very popular rock star, and everyone at Sweet Valley Middle School was crazy about him. The stands would be empty before the clock ran out.

And Elizabeth's rally was doomed.

The game was an exciting one, with a close score, but Elizabeth wasn't paying much attention to it. Sitting in the front row of the stands with Julie and Amy, she kept turning around and looking at the crowd behind her.

She shivered nervously. "Look at all the people!" She had to yell to be heard over the crowd.

"Think about all those votes," Julie yelled back, grinning. "Once they hear what you've got to say, you'll have them all on your side."

Elizabeth practiced her speech over and over. She'd spent the past two days memorizing it, and she thought she knew it by heart. The words rang in her head: "My name is Elizabeth Wakefield. I'm running for sixth-grade class president."

"Elizabeth, are you talking to yourself?" Amy asked curiously.

Elizabeth went red. She hadn't realized she was moving her lips. She turned and looked at the crowd again. It was funny—this time there didn't seem to be as many people. Maybe she was just feeling more confident.

"There's only a minute or two left," Julie said. "Are you ready?"

"As ready as I'll ever be," Elizabeth replied. Then, out of the corner of her eye, she noticed a group of kids climbing down from the stands and hurrying off in the direction of the parking lot.

"Excuse me," said a voice behind her. Elizabeth moved aside while three girls scrambled past her. She watched as they, too, seemed to be heading for the parking lot.

"Hey, the game's not over yet!" Amy called after them, but they didn't pay any attention.

Elizabeth turned around. Now there were only half as many people in the stands as there had been a minute ago.

"What's going on?" she asked Julie and Amy in bewilderment. But they were just as puzzled as she was.

Elizabeth looked down toward the end of her row. Something curious was happening. Ellen Riteman had gone up to a bunch of sixth-grade boys and was telling them something. Suddenly they all jumped up and took off.

All over the stands kids were leaving. And they all seemed to be going to the parking lot.

Just then she saw Kerry Glenn and Cammi Adams, two sixth-grade girls, walking past her.

"Kerry! Cammi! Where's everyone going?"

Kerry turned to her excitedly. "Haven't you heard? They're giving away Johnny Buck records in the parking lot!"

"Who's giving them away?" Elizabeth asked them. The girls were hurrying on, but their words drifted back to her.

"Lila and Jessica!"

Elizabeth froze. Lila and Jessica? Had she heard correctly?

"The game's over," Julie said softly. She didn't have to yell now. There was no noise in the stands.

Even the members of the soccer team were heading toward the parking lot.

Elizabeth just sat there in shock. Slowly she turned and surveyed the stands. There were only about ten kids still sitting there.

One of them was Randy Mason. He got up and came over to Elizabeth.

"Are you going to have your rally now?" he asked.

"What's the point?" Elizabeth replied dully.

"I'd like to hear what you have to say," Randy said. "I think it's important to know a candidate's plans."

"Go ahead," Amy encouraged her. "There are still a few kids here. It can't hurt."

Slowly, feeling like a robot, Elizabeth drew herself to her feet. She stepped down to the ground, turned, and faced the few kids remaining in the stands.

"My name is Elizabeth Wakefield," she said, her voice quavering. "I'm running for sixth-grade class president. If I'm elected, this is what I'll do. . . ."

By the time she got home that afternoon, Elizabeth was so depressed she felt like bursting into tears. How could her very own twin sister do something like this? She hadn't done anything to hurt Jessica's campaign. Why would Jessica go out of her way to ruin Elizabeth's rally?

She knew her expression reflected her feelings. Even her brother Steven noticed when she walked into the living room—and Steven wasn't the most sensitive person in the world.

"What's the matter with you?" he said.

"Where's Jessica?" Elizabeth asked.

"I don't know. Out somewhere, I guess." He looked at her with interest. "What did she do to you this time?"

Elizabeth plunked down on the sofa. "I was supposed to have a rally for my campaign after the soccer game. But everyone left even before the game was over. It turned out Jessica and Lila were giving away free Johnny Buck records in the parking lot."

Steven whistled. "Wow! She means business!"

Elizabeth didn't bother to respond. She just shrugged. "I just can't believe she'd do something like that to me."

Steven rolled his eyes and shook his head. "Elizabeth, you're such a wimp!"

Elizabeth stared at her brother. "What do you mean?" she exclaimed.

"You sound like you're ready to give up!"

Elizabeth was afraid she might start crying. "Maybe I *should* just drop out. There's no way I can win if Jessica keeps pulling these dirty tricks on me."

"Look," Steven said in a serious voice, "get your act together. If you want to win this election, you've got to fight fire with fire."

Elizabeth looked at him blankly. "I don't get it."

Steven sighed in exasperation. "You gotta play the game the way Jessica's playing it. If she's going to pull dirty tricks like this on you, you have to come up with some schemes of your own."

Elizabeth bit her lip. "What kind of schemes?"

Steven grinned. "I've got an idea. Come on, I'll show you something I found."

Elizabeth followed him out of the room and down to the basement. He led her into the laundry room.

"Look," he said, pointing to what looked like a stack of cardboard on top of the dryer.

Elizabeth picked one up and her eyes widened. It was a professionally-made poster. There was a photograph of Jessica on it, and above the picture it read: JESSICA WAKEFIELD FOR SIXTH-GRADE PRESIDENT.

"Where did Jessica get these?" Elizabeth asked in wonderment.

"Her friend Ellen has an uncle who owns a printing shop," Steven told her. "She's planning to put them up all over school on Monday."

Elizabeth stared at the posters in envy. These would definitely impress everyone. Elizabeth didn't stand a chance now.

"You know," Steven said slyly, "if something happened to these posters, Jessica wouldn't have enough time to get any more made before the election. Think about it, Elizabeth. Here's your big chance to get even."

With that he stuck his hands in his pockets and sauntered away.

Elizabeth stood there, still looking at the posters. It would be so easy to rip them to shreds. But she knew she just couldn't sink to Jessica's level.

Elizabeth left the laundry room and went upstairs to her bedroom. She sat at her desk and tried to think. Was there anything she could do to win this election? She'd tried flyers, but Jessica had ruined those. She'd tried a rally, but Jessica had ruined that, too.

The more she thought about Jessica, the angrier she became. She realized she wasn't just angry at Jessica—she was angry at herself, too. She was letting Jessica walk all over her! Steven was right. She *was* being a wimp!

She spotted a thick, black marking pen on her desk. For a second she just stared at it. And suddenly she knew what she was going to do.

She grabbed the pen and ran out of her room, down the stairs, and then down to the basement. She marched into the laundry room and set about getting her revenge.

When she was finished, she examined her work. On every poster there was Jessica's smiling face—with a thick black moustache drawn over her lips.

As she surveyed the posters, Elizabeth couldn't help but feel a little sick inside. Had she really done this? Then she thought about the flyers again, and the rally. *It serves her right,* she told herself firmly, and went back up to her room.

A few minutes later she heard Jessica come home. When she didn't come upstairs right away, Elizabeth knew she was probably going down to the basement to look at her posters. She sat stiffly on her bed and tried to prepare herself for what she knew was about to come.

A minute later Jessica burst into Elizabeth's room. Her face was bright red, and she was clutching one of the posters in her hand.

"Did you do this?" she cried furiously. "You ruined my posters!"

"Well, you ruined my rally!" Elizabeth shouted back. "And my flyers!"

"I didn't have anything to do with your flyers!"

Elizabeth jumped up and was just about to yell something back at her when she noticed her mother standing in the doorway.

"Girls! What's going on here?"

"Look at what Elizabeth did," Jessica said angrily.

Mrs. Wakefield looked at the poster and her eyebrows went up. "Elizabeth, did you really do this? This is terrible! I'm very surprised at you!"

"You should hear what she did to me!" Elizabeth exclaimed. "First she dumped all my flyers into the school fountain. Then she made sure nobody would be at my rally!"

"I did not dump your stupid flyers in the fountain!" Jessica yelled.

"Yes, you did!"

"No, I didn't!"

"Girls, girls!" Now Mrs. Wakefield was looking very upset. "Stop it, right this minute!"

They stopped yelling, but Elizabeth's fists were clenched, and Jessica's eyes were blazing. Mrs. Wakefield sat down on Elizabeth's bed.

"I was afraid something like this would happen," she said wearily. "I thought you girls were grown-up enough to handle a competition. It seems I was wrong."

Neither of the twins said anything. They just stood there, glaring at each other.

"I think perhaps you should both drop out of this election," Mrs. Wakefield said.

"Drop out!" Jessica wailed. "I can't drop out! I'm going to win!"

Their mother sighed. "I don't like these fights. This is not the way sisters should behave."

"We won't fight anymore," Jessica said quickly.

"And I don't want to hear about any more nasty little tricks," Mrs. Wakefield added. She fixed her eyes sternly on Elizabeth.

Elizabeth could barely bring herself to meet her mother's gaze. "No more tricks," she said softly.

"I'm going to say this once, and I'm not going to say it again," their mother continued. "I don't want to hear one more argument about this campaign. If you can't go about this business in a mature and civilized way, you will both have to drop out of the election. Is that clear?"

Both girls nodded.

"All right," Mrs. Wakefield said, getting up. "Now, come down to the kitchen and help me with dinner." She walked out of the room, and Elizabeth got up to follow her.

Jessica handed her the poster. "Here," she said coldly. "You can have this for a souvenir." Tossing her head, she turned and walked out of the room.

Elizabeth took one last look at the poster. Then, feeling very sad, she folded it up and threw it in the wastebasket.

Eight

◇

Elizabeth and Jessica barely spoke to each other all weekend. In front of their parents, at the dinner table, they would say things like "Pass the salt, please," but the rest of the time they avoided each other. They spent most of the weekend seeing their own friends, and when they were at home, they each stayed in their own bedrooms.

By Sunday Elizabeth felt confused and upset. She hated having these bad feelings about Jessica. That afternoon she went over to Amy's to talk about it.

"I think maybe I should just drop out, and let Jessica win the election," she told her friend.

"That's crazy," Amy objected. "That's just giving in to her. It's about time Jessica learned she can't always get her own way."

"I know," Elizabeth said. "But she's probably going to win anyway."

"Maybe," Amy said. "But you shouldn't make it so easy for her. Besides, if you drop out, you'll just get a reputation for being a quitter."

Elizabeth thought about that. "You're right," she said finally. "It would be one thing if I dropped out because Jessica was the better candidate. But she's not! I know I'd be a better class president than she would."

Amy agreed. "Absolutely! Not to mention the fact that Ms. Luster is counting on getting that VCR with the money from the book fair."

"Do you honestly think I have a chance of winning?" Elizabeth asked her.

"I *think* so," Amy said slowly. "Of course, those free records will probably help Jessica. But when we have the assembly on Tuesday, you'll get another chance to tell the class what you'll do as president. I think then the kids will see that you'd be much better than Jessica."

"I hope so," Elizabeth said. But she wasn't feeling very confident.

At school on Monday she tried to talk to as many students as she could. By lunchtime she was feeling a little bit better. Several kids had told her they liked the idea of buying a VCR for the library. But others said they preferred the idea of having a party. It seemed to her that she and Jessica each had about the same number of votes. It was impossible to tell who would end up winning.

Amy and Julie were waiting for her outside the cafeteria. Julie was studying something tacked to the bulletin board.

"Look at this," she said to Elizabeth.

It was a computer printout. The letters were so small and light, Elizabeth could barely read it.

"If you want to hear what Randy Mason will do for you, come to a rally after school today," she read aloud. She shook her head sadly. "Poor Randy. He still thinks he's got a real chance to win."

"He'll probably say he wants to spend the book fair money on computer equipment," Julie said. "And since we've already got loads of that stuff, I don't think anyone's going to get too excited about that idea."

"I wonder if anyone will actually show up for his rally," Amy said.

Elizabeth looked at the notice again. "I think we should go," she said. "After all, he came to my rally."

"That's OK with me," Amy said. "At least he'll have three people to speak to."

Amy was almost right. Actually, there were five at the rally—the three girls, plus two boys who were friends of Randy's. When the girls arrived, Randy was telling the boys that if he became president, he'd put all the school activities into the computer system. Then, when kids wanted to know what was going on each day, they could hit a button on one of the school's computer terminals and find out.

"For example," Randy said, "if someone were

interested in stamp collecting, they could type on the computer keyboard and find out when the stamp collectors club meets."

"I didn't even know there *was* a stamp collectors club," Amy whispered to Elizabeth.

Elizabeth found a lot of what Randy had to say was pretty interesting. He had a really good idea for a sixth-grade charity project. He thought the class could take up a collection to sponsor a child in a foreign country.

"The whole sixth grade could be foster parents for some needy child," he said enthusiastically.

He also had ideas for new school activities. "Sports are great," he said. "But I think there should be more competitive activities for kids who don't like physical sports. Maybe we could start championship chess matches or Scrabble contests."

"Those are good ideas," Elizabeth whispered to her friends. "You know, I don't think he's such a nerd after all."

Julie raised her hand. "Randy, what do you think should be done with the money the sixth grade will make from the book fair?"

"I've been thinking about that," Randy said. "I know Jessica Wakefield says we should spend the money on a big party." He turned to Elizabeth. "And Elizabeth, you think we should spend it on a VCR for the library. Right?"

"Right," Elizabeth said. "What do you think we should spend the money on?"

"I think we should have both."

"What?" Elizabeth stared at him. Maybe Randy wasn't as smart as she had thought. "We don't have enough money to do both!"

"We will if we do it this way," Randy said. "First, we spend the money on a big party."

"But then there won't be money for a VCR," Elizabeth interrupted.

"Yes, there will," Randy continued, smiling. "*If* we charge money to go to the party! See, it works like this: The sixth grade sponsors the party, but the students have to buy tickets if they want to go. Then we use the ticket money to buy the VCR for the library!"

Elizabeth gasped. It was so simple! Why hadn't she thought of that?

"That's a fantastic idea," she said to Julie and Amy as they walked home.

"No kidding," Amy said. "That way, everyone would be happy."

"It's the perfect solution," Julie agreed. "All the kids will love it."

"Elizabeth, why don't you suggest that idea tomorrow at the assembly?" Amy suggested.

"I can't do that," Elizabeth objected. "It's Randy's idea."

"OK, maybe Randy thought of it first," Amy said. "But you know he doesn't have a chance of winning."

"Amy's right," Julie said. "I think the votes are

pretty evenly split between you and Jessica. If you say you'll spend the money on a party *and* a VCR, that could bring a lot more votes to your side."

Elizabeth considered Julie's idea for a minute. "I guess I could tell the audience it's Randy's idea, but if I'm elected, I'll spend the money that way, too."

She was still thinking it over when she got home. Randy's idea plus her own popularity would definitely give her the edge over Jessica. But was it fair to Randy?

Randy couldn't possibly beat both Elizabeth and Jessica. So if Elizabeth didn't present his idea, and Jessica won, then the class would only get the party.

Elizabeth was totally confused. She needed to talk this out with someone, so she was very happy to find her mother reading the newspaper at the kitchen table.

Elizabeth sat down next to her mother. "I've got a problem with this campaign," she told her.

Mrs. Wakefield sighed. "Elizabeth, are you and Jessica at it again? I told you—"

"It's got nothing to do with Jessica," Elizabeth said quickly. She told her mother about Randy's idea for the book fair money.

"That's a very good plan," Mrs. Wakefield said. "I suppose that means Randy will win the election. Is that why you're upset?"

Elizabeth shook her head. "Randy can't win this election, even with the best idea. He's not very popular. In fact, most of the kids don't like him."

"That's too bad," said Mrs. Wakefield. "Especially if his idea is the best one."

"It *is* the best idea," Elizabeth said. "And I think that if I tell the sixth graders that's the way I'll spend the money, too, I could win."

"But wouldn't that be stealing Randy's idea?" her mother asked.

"Not exactly," Elizabeth said. "I mean, I'd tell everyone it was his idea. I wouldn't try to pretend I thought of it myself."

"I don't know, Elizabeth," her mother said, shaking her head. "It doesn't feel right to me."

Elizabeth nodded reluctantly. "I know. It doesn't feel right to me either. But I know Randy won't win, no matter how good his ideas are. And if I say I'll do the same thing, and I win, the whole school will benefit."

"And if you don't take Randy's idea, what will happen then?" Mrs. Wakefield asked.

Elizabeth sighed. "If Jessica wins, all they'll get is a costume party."

Her mother smiled sympathetically. "I know it's a hard decision to make, Elizabeth. And I wish I could tell you what to do. But it's your decision, and I think it's something you should handle on your own." She reached out and patted Elizabeth's hand. "Honey, I know it's not easy, trying to figure out the right thing to do. But it's all part of growing up. Just think about it for a while, and I'm sure you'll realize what you have to do."

Elizabeth had a feeling that that was what her mother was going to say. And deep in her heart, she knew her mother was right. It was her decision to make. But how should she make it? What was the right thing to do?

"OK, Mom," she said. "I'll think about it."

She was still sitting at the kitchen table, alone, when Jessica came walking in a half hour later. She walked directly to the refrigerator without speaking to Elizabeth, took out an apple, then started to leave.

"Jessica, wait," Elizabeth said.

"What do you want?" Jessica asked coldly.

Elizabeth took a deep breath. "Look, I'm really sorry about marking up your posters."

Jessica looked surprised. "You are?"

Elizabeth nodded. "Yeah. It was a pretty nasty thing for me to do."

Jessica shrugged, and turned as if to walk out of the room. She paused at the doorway, though, and turned around. "I'm sorry about messing up your rally," she said.

Apologies didn't come easy to her, and she didn't sound terribly sincere, but Elizabeth didn't mind. At least Jessica was making an effort to get along.

"It was actually Lila's idea," Jessica added hastily. A slightly abashed grin crossed her face. "But I guess I shouldn't have gone along with it."

"What about the flyers?" Elizabeth asked. "Who's idea was that?"

"Honestly, Lizzie, I had nothing to do with that. It was Ellen. She found the flyers in the library and threw them in the fountain."

"Oh." This time Elizabeth actually believed her. She put her elbows on the table and her chin in her hands. "We've both been acting awfully silly."

"Yeah, I guess so," Jessica said, pulling up a chair and joining her. "But I still want to win this election."

Elizabeth nodded. "So do I."

"Just think," Jessica said dreamily. "Tomorrow at this time one of us will be the sixth-grade class president."

"I know," Elizabeth said. "But which one?" She smiled at her twin. "No matter which of us wins, we'll still be like we've always been. Not just sisters, but best friends, too. Right?"

"Right," Jessica replied. "Just don't go putting any more moustaches on my pictures, OK?"

Elizabeth felt ashamed. "That was a pretty nasty thing for me to do, wasn't it?"

Jessica's eyes were sparkling. "Oh, I don't know about that. It sounds exactly like the kind of thing I'd do."

And for the first time in a while, both twins burst out laughing.

Nine

"Jessica! Aren't you ready yet?"

Elizabeth stood in the entrance to Jessica's bedroom with her hands on her hips. Jessica was wearing only her slip and standing in the middle of a pile of clothes.

"I don't know what to wear!" Jessica wailed. "I'm going to give a speech in front of the entire sixth grade, and I've got to look fabulous!"

Elizabeth marched over to the pile of discarded outfits and pulled out a dark pink jersey dress. "Wear this," she ordered.

"It's not bright enough," Jessica complained. "I want to stand out on the stage."

Elizabeth opened a drawer in Jessica's bureau

and extracted a purple sash. "Wear this with it," she suggested. "This is definitely bright."

Jessica looked at it doubtfully. "Purple with pink? Do you think it goes together?"

"It's a major fashion statement," Elizabeth said firmly. "I, uh . . . saw something exactly like it in this month's issue of *Teen Styles*." That wasn't exactly true, but Elizabeth thought it sounded good.

"OK," Jessica said, and took the sash from Elizabeth. Then she gasped. "I can't wear this! You're wearing orange. We'll clash."

Elizabeth groaned. "Then we'll sit with Randy in between us."

"Who?"

"Randy Mason, dummy! The other candidate!"

"Oh, yeah." Jessica pulled on the pink dress. "I keep forgetting about him." She went over to the mirror. "How should I fix my hair?"

"Jess, just hurry up! We can't be late today." Elizabeth tried hard not to sound too impatient, but watching her sister fuss like this was making her feel uncomfortable. Because she knew—at least she had a pretty strong suspicion—that Jessica wasn't going to win the election. Not if Elizabeth went ahead and did what she was thinking about doing.

When they arrived at school, the twins headed directly for the auditorium. Once again the entire sixth grade was filing in.

Jessica called and waved to everyone in sight, but Elizabeth could barely bring herself to smile—

her stomach was in knots. She was glad she was walking with her sister. Whenever she was really nervous about something, there was no one she'd rather be with than Jessica. And she wanted to stay as close to her as possible. Right now they were on good terms with each other, but after this assembly, Jessica might never speak to her again.

Amy ran over to Elizabeth and pinched her. "That's for good luck!" she said.

Elizabeth smiled weakly. "Thanks," she managed to say. But luck wasn't what she needed. What she needed today was courage.

Once again Mr. Bowman climbed up to the stage. "Get a load of that outfit," Jessica whispered to Elizabeth, giggling.

The teacher was wearing a plaid jacket with a green shirt, and a tie that looked like it contained every color in the rainbow.

It was pretty awful, Elizabeth had to admit. "And you were worried about clashing with *me*!" she whispered back.

On the stage next to Mr. Bowman there was a podium and three empty chairs. Elizabeth had a pretty good idea who they were for.

Sure enough, as everyone took a seat, Mr. Bowman called out, "Will the three candidates please come up here."

As Jessica and Elizabeth made their way onto the stage, Elizabeth could hear a group of kids chanting, "Jessica! Jessica! Jessica!" Immediately, another group started yelling, "Elizabeth! Elizabeth! Elizabeth!"

Elizabeth turned and saw Randy Mason following them up to the stage. He didn't look the least bit bothered by the fact that nobody was chanting *his* name.

They sat down—Randy at one end, Jessica and Elizabeth next to each other. Suddenly Jessica jumped up and asked Randy something. Randy looked a little puzzled, but he got up and changed seats with her. Elizabeth almost started laughing. With all the tension of the situation, Jessica was still concerned that she and Elizabeth might clash!

"OK, everyone, let's settle down," Mr. Bowman said into the microphone on the podium. The room got quiet as the sixth graders turned to him with expressions of eager anticipation. Elizabeth's eyes scanned the room. She saw Amy, looking excited and happy. And there was Julie, giving her a V for Victory signal. She hoped she wouldn't be letting them down.

"As you all know," Mr. Bowman said, "today you will be electing your new class president. Each candidate will speak to you about his or her plans for the year. Following each speech, you will have an opportunity to ask them questions. First, I will introduce all the candidates."

He turned and smiled at the three of them. "On the right, Jessica Wakefield."

The room burst into applause and cheers of

"Jessica! Jessica! Jessica!" Mr. Bowman had to hold up his hand to get the room quiet again.

"On the left is Elizabeth Wakefield."

Elizabeth was pleased to hear just as much applause and cheering as there had been for Jessica.

"And in the middle, Randy Mason."

This time there was only a smattering of applause, and no one called out Randy's name. But no one was rude either.

"The first candidate to speak is Jessica Wakefield."

Jessica bounced up from her seat and sauntered over to the podium. Elizabeth marveled at how cool and confident she seemed. When she got to the podium, Jessica tossed her head so her blond curls bobbed around her shoulders, then she flashed a brilliant smile at the audience.

"As you all know," Jessica said brightly, "we're going to have a book fair and make lots of money. If I'm elected sixth-grade class president, we'll spend that money on a fantastic party."

She stopped then, and just stood there smiling, as if she were waiting for some more applause.

"Is that all you have to say?" Mr. Bowman asked.

Jessica looked at him uncertainly. Then she turned back to the audience.

"Like I said, it'll be an unbelievably super party. Everyone has to come dressed as their favorite character from a book. If you don't like to read, you can come as your favorite character from a movie. But not from a television show."

"Why not?" someone yelled out from the audience.

Jessica grinned. "I don't know. I just figured there ought to be some rules."

Listening to Jessica speak, Elizabeth tried to hide her smile. Jessica didn't have the slightest idea what a class president had to do. She figured she could win the election on charm alone. And she was definitely charming. Elizabeth hoped that for once Jessica's charm wouldn't be enough.

"Have you anything more to say, Jessica?" Mr. Bowman asked.

"Nope, that's it!"

The teacher looked out at the sixth graders. "Are there any questions for Jessica?"

Amy jumped up. "I'd like to ask Jessica what else she'll do as sixth-grade president."

Jessica stared at her blankly. "Huh?"

"What are you going to do besides spend the book fair money on a costume party?"

"Gee, I don't know," Jessica said, looking a little flustered. "Whatever sixth-grade presidents are supposed to do, I guess." She paused, then added, "As long as it doesn't take too much time . . ."

With that, she offered one more bright smile and returned to her seat.

Mr. Bowman looked a little amused. Then he

addressed the class again. "Our next speaker is Elizabeth Wakefield."

Somehow Elizabeth managed to pull herself up and make it to the podium. If she was just going to make the campaign speech she had originally planned, she'd be feeling much more confident. But what she had to say wasn't going to be so easy.

She was almost surprised to hear her own voice coming out so calmly. "I decided to run for sixth-grade class president because I had an idea for the book fair money, too. I thought we should spend the money on a VCR for the library. I still think that's a good idea. But Randy Mason has an even better idea."

She paused and took a deep breath. "That's why I am going to drop out of the race."

A gasp went through the room. Elizabeth couldn't even bring herself to look at Amy's or Julie's faces.

"I'm sure Randy will be telling you about his idea," she continued. "And I hope you'll all agree with me that his plan is the best. I also hope that all of you who were going to vote for me will vote for Randy instead. Thank you."

By now the whole audience was buzzing. Elizabeth started to head back to her chair, then realized that if she wasn't a candidate anymore, she had no business being up there. So instead she stepped down from the stage and took a seat in the audience.

"Wow," the girl sitting next to her whispered. "That took real guts."

Elizabeth smiled and said thanks. But her smile faded when she caught Jessica's expression back up on the stage. Jessica looked completely shocked.

Mr. Bowman seemed pretty surprised, too. But once the audience had quieted down, he spoke again. "Next, we will hear from Randy Mason."

Randy looked poised as he made his way to the podium. And when he spoke, he sounded very self-assured.

"First of all, I want to thank Elizabeth for her support. I'm glad she likes my idea for the book fair money, and I hope you all will, too."

Randy described his plan to use the money for a party, charge admission, and use that money to buy a VCR for the library. "This way," he said, "we can have something fun and something useful, too."

He went on to talk about his other ideas—the daily activities printout and sponsoring a child overseas. As Elizabeth looked around the quiet auditorium, she could tell that everyone was actually listening.

She did hear one boy whispering to another behind her. "You know, I always thought that guy was a real nerd. But he's kind of sharp."

Elizabeth recognized the voice of the boy responding to him. "I nominated him, you know," Jim Sturbridge bragged.

When Randy finished his speech, lots of kids

had questions for him—like what he would do to help raise sixth-grade school spirit, and how to get more people involved in school activities. For each question, Randy responded with a thoughtful, intelligent comment.

As he returned to his seat, Elizabeth looked to see how her sister was reacting. Jessica was scowling, and Elizabeth felt more than a little sorry for her. She thought she'd better feel sorry for herself, too—Jessica must be furious with her. But still, she had no regrets for what she'd done.

Mr. Bowman went up to the podium. "We will now vote by secret ballot. Write down your vote, then pass your ballots forward."

As Elizabeth waited for her ballot, she felt a hand on her shoulder. When she turned, she saw Amy huddled down in the row behind her.

"Why did you do that?" Amy asked.

Elizabeth smiled. "He had the best idea, and he ought to win. But I knew he couldn't win against both me and Jessica. So I figured by dropping out and throwing him my votes, he might have a chance."

"Yes, I guess you're right," Amy said. "Are you going to vote for him over Jessica?"

Elizabeth hadn't even thought about that. Amy hurried back to her seat, and Elizabeth found herself holding a stack of ballots, taking one, and passing them on.

Now what? On the one hand, Jessica was Elizabeth's own twin sister . . . but on the other hand, Elizabeth knew who'd make the better class president. And even with his great platform, against Jessica's popularity Randy needed all the help he could get.

Feeling a little bit like a traitor, and glancing around to make sure no one was looking, she scribbled *Randy Mason* on her ballot. Then she folded it and refolded it.

The sixth-grade teachers came down the aisles and collected the ballots. Mr. Bowman put them into a basket and announced that he'd take them backstage for counting.

The minute he disappeared, students began getting out of their seats and gathering in little groups. Randy came down from the stage, and he was immediately surrounded by a small group of kids. Elizabeth felt a little sick as she saw Jessica leave the stage and start toward her. Luckily, though, Lila and Ellen pulled her aside.

But it was only a temporary reprieve, Elizabeth knew. Sooner or later she'd have to face Jessica. She'd just rather it be later.

A few minutes went by before Mr. Bowman returned to the stage. Everyone rushed back to their seats.

"We have a winner," Mr. Bowman announced. A hush came over the crowd.

"The new sixth grade president is . . ." He paused for dramatic effect. "Randy Mason!"

Ten

◇

Elizabeth had mixed feelings when she arrived home from school that afternoon. She was still proud of what she had done. Randy Mason was going to be a terrific class president. He was so pleased and happy about his election that it made her feel really good about helping him win.

After school Randy had asked her if she'd like to be "special executive assistant" to the president. She wasn't sure what that meant, but it certainly sounded important. So she was feeling pretty good about that, too.

But Elizabeth knew she still had to face Jessica. Somehow she'd managed to avoid her all day at school. That wasn't too hard—every time she saw

Jessica, she was surrounded by sympathetic, consol-
ing Unicorns.

But now Elizabeth was home. She hoped Jessica
wouldn't be there yet—but that hope was dashed the
minute she walked through the door.

Steven was in the kitchen, eating as usual. "I
guess you won the election," he said between
mouthfuls.

"No, I didn't win. I dropped out," Elizabeth
said. "Randy Mason won. Why did you think I
did?"

Steven looked surprised. "Because Jessica came
storming in the house like a tornado and went
straight up to her room. I figured you must have
beaten her."

Elizabeth shook her head. "No, but I guess I
had something to do with Randy winning."

"Well, I'd watch out if I were you," Steven said.
"From the way she was moving, I wouldn't want to
get in her way."

"Thanks for the warning," Elizabeth said
weakly. She left the kitchen and went upstairs to her
room, trying to be as quiet as possible. Maybe she
could manage to hide until dinner.

But she'd been in her room less than a minute
when her door burst open and Jessica rushed in.
Elizabeth's eyes were fixed on the floor.

"Lizzie!"

Elizabeth raised her eyes reluctantly, expecting

to confront the angriest face she'd ever encountered. But to her amazement, that wasn't what she saw.

Jessica was grinning from ear to ear. In one hand she clutched a battered book.

"I've got it!" she said gleefully.

Elizabeth looked at her in bewilderment. "Got what?"

Jessica thrust the book toward her. "I figured out what you can be for the costume party!"

Elizabeth took the book from her. It was the twins' old copy of *Alice in Wonderland*. Jessica pointed to an illustration.

"You can be Alice! We can do your hair like this, and find a cute little pinafore."

"That's a good idea," Elizabeth said. "This was always one of my favorite books when I was little."

Jessica looked very pleased with herself. "I'm going to have to help a lot of kids with this. Randy asked me to be in charge of organizing the party."

"Really? That's great!" Elizabeth said sincerely.

"I've got to get right to work," Jessica continued. "I have to set up a committee for decorations, and another one for refreshments."

As she started out of the room, Elizabeth stopped her. "Jess," she said, "aren't you angry about what I did in the assembly?"

Jessica paused. "Well, I think it was a pretty dumb thing to do. But I guess it worked out OK. I just found out class presidents have meetings almost every week! I wouldn't even have time for my ballet classes!" And with that she danced happily out of the room.

At dinner that evening Elizabeth told the whole family what had happened. Only Steven looked disappointed. "I was sort of looking forward to the featherweight championship battle of the century."

"Well, we're proud of you, Elizabeth," Mr. Wakefield said. "We're proud of both of you! Elizabeth did something very noble, and Jessica, you seem to be taking your defeat very well."

"I probably could have won if I really wanted to," Jessica said. "But all those meetings! Yuck."

Mrs. Wakefield smiled at Elizabeth. "I'm sure that wasn't an easy decision for you to make, honey. I know you really wanted to be class president."

Elizabeth nodded. "But I know I did the right thing. And that's just as good as winning."

Jessica's eyebrows went up. "It is?"

Elizabeth grinned. "Well . . . almost!"

Eleven

◇

Jessica was sitting in front of the television on Saturday afternoon when Elizabeth walked into the den.

"What are you watching?" Elizabeth asked her.

"Music videos," Jessica replied without removing her eyes from the screen. "Look at that singer. Isn't he amazing?"

Elizabeth looked at the TV. "He's cute," she agreed.

"Cute? He's gorgeous!" Jessica sighed. "I wish I could meet a boy like that."

"He's not a boy, Jess," Elizabeth said. "He's a man. He must be at least twenty."

"Yeah, I guess he *is* kind of old," Jessica admitted. "But boys our age are so—I don't know . . .

childish. I wish I could meet an older boy." She grinned at Elizabeth. "Wouldn't it be neat to go out with a sixteen-year-old boy? He'd be able to drive."

"But I don't think many sixteen-year-old boys want to date twelve-year-old girls," Elizabeth noted.

"I suppose not." Jessica got up and looked at herself in a mirror. "Don't you think I could pass for someone older? Like maybe fourteen?"

Elizabeth looked at her suspiciously. "OK, Jessica, what are you up to now?"

Jessica laughed. "Don't be silly, Lizzie. I don't even know any sixteen-year-old boys. Listen, do you want to go to the skating rink? I'm meeting Lila there."

Elizabeth hesitated. Amy was going to come over a little later, but the two of them hadn't made any plans. Roller skating sounded like fun.

"I'm not sure," she replied. "Maybe Amy and I will come."

Jessica ran upstairs to brush her hair and pick out the perfect outfit for roller skating. That took longer than she had planned, and by the time she rode her bike to the rink, she was fifteen minutes late.

Putting on her skates, she spotted Lila way over on the other side of the rink. She quickly finished lacing up the skates, and took off.

She was skating faster than usual, trying to catch up with Lila. With all the other kids skating around her, she had to dodge around and between them. She was doing pretty well until another girl darted in front of her. Then Jessica lost her balance and started to fall.

But before she could hit the ground, a strong hand grabbed her arm and hoisted her up.

"Thanks," Jessica said, and looked up to see her rescuer. She practically gasped.

The person who had helped her had to be one of the best-looking boys she'd ever seen. His Sweet Valley High T-shirt revealed tanned, muscular arms. He had wavy blond hair, and eyes so green they could have been traffic lights.

"Are you okay?" the boy asked, sounding concerned. "You almost took a bad fall just now."

Jessica hoped she wasn't blushing. She must have looked like an idiot, she thought, practically tripping over her own feet. And right in front of the most gorgeous boy on earth. He had to be even cuter than that rock star on TV.

"I'm OK," she managed to say. "But if you hadn't caught me, I might have broken a leg or something."

"You were going pretty fast," he said. "Where's the fire?"

Jessica laughed lightly, and tossed her head so her hair would bounce around her shoulders. "No fire. I was just trying to catch up with my friend."

He raised his eyebrows. "Boyfriend?"

"Oh, no," Jessica said hastily. "Just a girlfriend."

"That's good," he said, and his brown eyes sparkled.

Jessica couldn't believe it—he was actually flirting with her! And now that she'd had a chance to look at him more carefully, she knew he had to be a teenager—at least fifteen, maybe even older!

"I'm Josh Angler," he said. "I haven't seen you around Sweet Valley High. Are you new in town?"

Before Jessica could reply, a voice behind her called, "Jessica! There you are!"

Jessica turned and saw Lila on the sidelines, her hands on her hips. She didn't look very happy.

"I'll be right there," Jessica called. She turned to Josh. "I guess I'd better go meet my friend."

"Well, at least I know your name now," Josh said. "Are you going to be around for a while?"

"Sure," Jessica said. She could feel her heart beating wildly. Josh had a wonderful smile.

"Then maybe we could have a soda later," he suggested.

Jessica tossed her head again. "OK."

"Jessica!" Lila's voice was louder and more insistent.

"See you later," Jessica told Josh, and turned to skate toward Lila.

"Try and stay on your feet now," he called after her.

Jessica felt as if her feet would never touch the ground again.

"Who were you talking to?" Lila asked as Jessica skated closer.

"His name's Josh," Jessica said. "He caught me when I almost fell. Isn't he cute?" She giggled. "I think he likes me. He wants to have a soda later."

"You're kidding!" Lila looked really surprised. "He looks old to me."

"He is," Jessica said. "He goes to Sweet Valley High."

Lila sniffed. "Well, he might like you now, but wait till he finds out you're only twelve years old."

Jessica shrugged and grinned slyly. "Maybe he doesn't have to find out."

"What do you mean?" Lila asked, her eyes narrowing.

Jessica just laughed. "C'mon," she said. "Let's skate." And she took off, leaving Lila standing there with her mouth open.

Will Josh Angler be that perfect "older boy" that Jessica has been dreaming about? Find out in Sweet Valley Twins #15, **THE OLDER BOY.**

Get Ready for a Thrilling Time in Sweet Valley®!

☐ **26905 DOUBLE JEOPARDY #1**   **$2.95**

When the twins get part-time jobs on the Sweet Valley newspaper, they're in for some chilling turn of events. The "scoops" Jessica invents to impress a college reporter turn into the real thing when she witnesses an actual crime—but now no one will believe her! The criminal has seen her car, and now he's going after Elizabeth ... the twins have faced danger and adventure before ... but never like this!

Watch for the second Sweet Valley Thriller

SWEET VALLEY HIGH

☐	26741	DOUBLE LOVE #1	$2.75
☐	26621	SECRETS #2	$2.75
☐	27669	PLAYING WITH FIRE #3	$2.95
☐	27493	POWER PLAY #4	$2.95
☐	26742	ALL NIGHT LONG #5	$2.75
☐	26813	DANGEROUS LOVE #6	$2.75
☐	27672	DEAR SISTER #7	$2.95
☐	26744	HEARTBREAKER #8	$2.75
☐	26626	RACING HEARTS #9	$2.75
☐	27668	WRONG KIND OF GIRL #10	$2.95
☐	26824	TOO GOOD TO BE TRUE #11	$2.75
☐	26688	WHEN LOVE DIES #12	$2.75
☐	26619	KIDNAPPED #13	$2.75
☐	26764	DECEPTIONS #14	$2.75
☐	26765	PROMISES #15	$2.75
☐	27431	RAGS TO RICHES #16	$2.95
☐	26883	LOVE LETTERS #17	$2.75
☐	27444	HEAD OVER HEELS #18	$2.95
☐	27589	SHOWDOWN #19	$2.95
☐	26959	CRASH LANDING! #20	$2.75
☐	26682	RUNAWAY #21	$2.75
☐	26745	TOO MUCH IN LOVE #22	$2.75
☐	26689	SAY GOODBYE #23	$2.75
☐	26684	MEMORIES #24	$2.75

Prices and availability subject to change without notice.

Buy them at your local bookstore or use this page to order

- -

Celebrate the Seasons
with SWEET VALLEY HIGH
Super Editions

You've been a SWEET VALLEY HIGH fan all along—hanging out with Jessica and Elizabeth and their friends at Sweet Valley High. And now the SWEET VALLEY HIGH *Super Editions* give you more of what you like best—more romance—more excitement—more real-life adventure! Whether you're bicycling up the California Coast in PERFECT SUMMER, dancing at the Sweet Valley Christmas Ball in SPECIAL CHRISTMAS, touring the South of France in SPRING BREAK, catching the rays in a MALIBU SUMMER, or skiing the snowy slopes in WINTER CARNIVAL—you know you're exactly where you want to be—with the gang from SWEET VALLEY HIGH.

SWEET VALLEY HIGH SUPER EDITIONS

☐ PERFECT SUMMER
25072/$2.95

☐ SPRING BREAK
25537/$2.95

☐ SPECIAL CHRISTMAS
25377/$2.95

☐ MALIBU SUMMER
26050/$2.95

☐ WINTER CARNIVAL
26159/$2.95

☐ SPRING FEVER
26420/$2.95

Prices and availability subject to change without notice.